SHE WHO BINDS THE FAE PRINCE

K. Malady

Also By

THE ASCEND TRIALS
YA fantasy romance adventure

THE HARMONY CHRONICLES
NA paranormal romance/contemporary
fantasy

THREADS OF FATE
NA/Adult romantic fantasy retellings

KNEELING KINGDOMS
Adult interconnected standalone romantasy

Avalaruin
Council house
Bridge
Ti

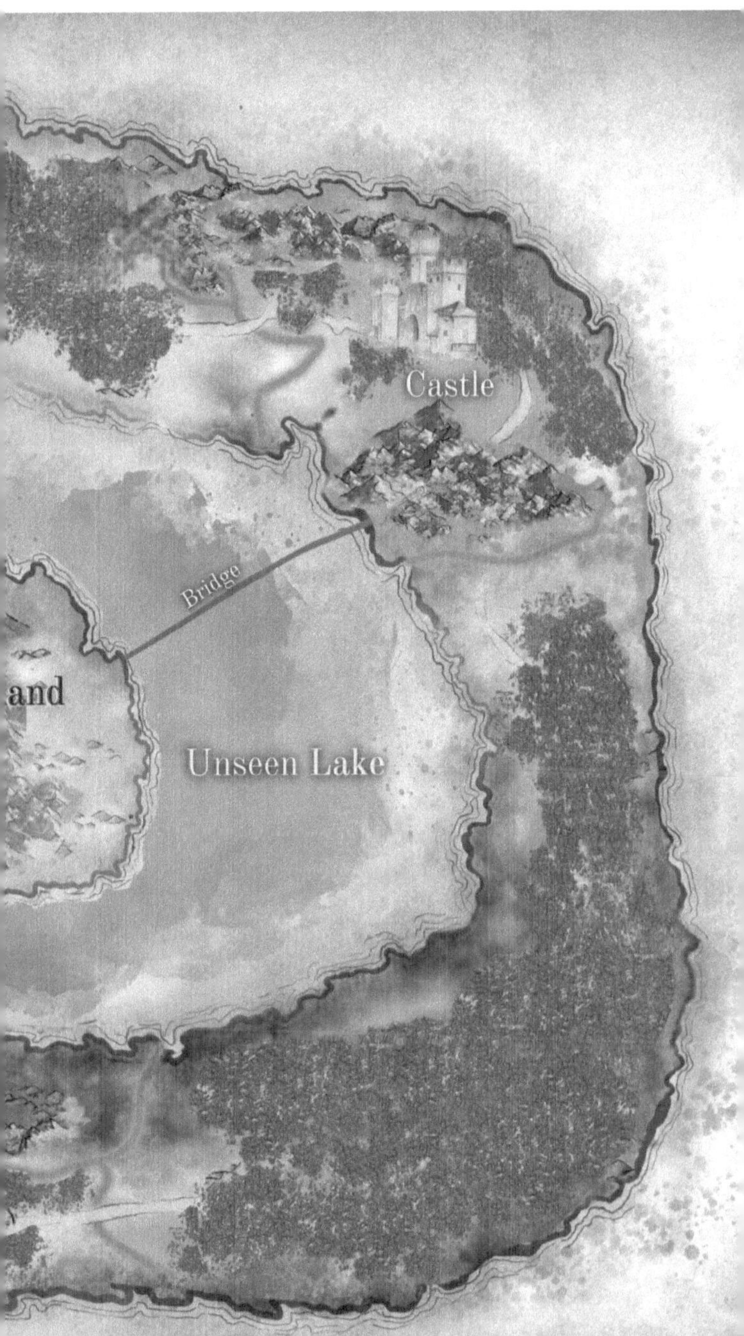
Castle
Bridge
and
Unseen Lake

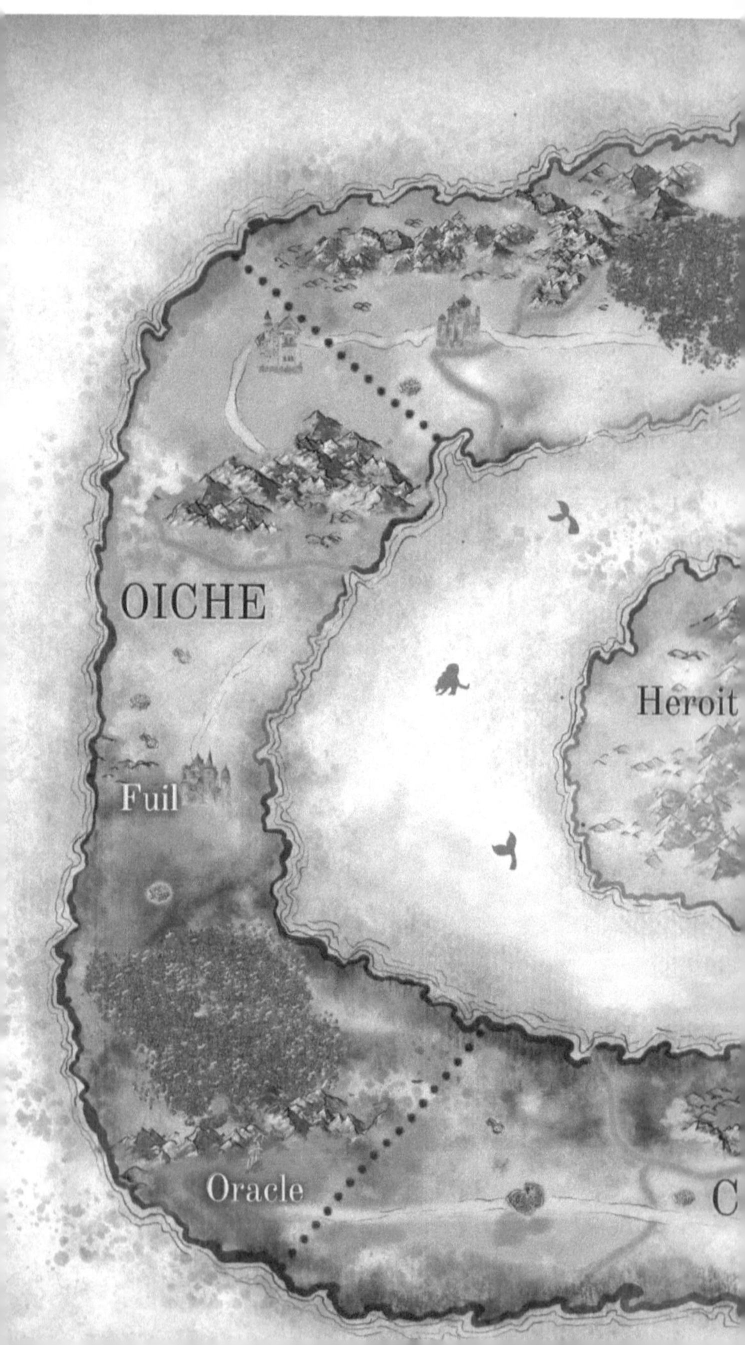

OICHE
Fuil
Oracle
Heroit
C

The
Aboveground
THA
EALACH
Prism Lake
THA
AN

Chapter 1

THE MOON HANGS AS a mere sliver, almost swallowed by the inky night sky, as I kneel on the blanket in my makeshift ritual space deep within the forest near my home. The first light of dawn will break through the horizon soon, leaving me precious seconds to perfect this damned charm.

Like all fae, I have magic, but mine has a tendency to... misbehave. Most fae wield multiple types of magic—illusion, wishcraft, nature magic. Me? Just charms, and half the time my charms don't stick. I grew up under the whispered suspicions that I was a changeling or part-human because of my unreliable magical skills. Others guessed I might be a werewolf on my father's side, to account for my unruly bush of mousy brown hair.

It's possible, since I don't know my father, and actually a kinder suggestion than it sounds. It was certainly better than outright dismissals of my competence as a fae practitioner. Which, with my track record, would be an accurate statement, no matter how cruel.

But tonight, I've done everything I can to make this enchantment work. Before me is a small bowl of crystal-clear spring water, a handful of dried lavender, a silver feather, a piece of obsidian, and a vial of my blood. Each item was carefully chosen for its magical properties: the water for purity, the lavender for concealment, the feather for light-ness, the obsidian for protection, and the blood for a personal connection to the spell. And I'd gone overboard in my preparation, using the finest lavender picked at its peak potency, my blood drawn with the sharpest knife gleaming like liquid silver under the moonlight. Even the charm itself was penned with painstaking precision, using my best quill on high-quality parchment. I couldn't leave anything to chance if I wanted to escape the betrothal lists and remain in Avalaruin, the fae world.

The problem is that tonight is Beltane—which starts the clock where every unmarried fae must find a partner to bind with during Lughnasadh in three months. The binding lasts for a year and a day, after which partners may choose either to remain bound or go their separate ways. Each fae gets five chances before the binding becomes irrevocable. At twenty-eight years old, I'm staring down my fifth and final binding, having endured four disastrous unions already.

Oh sure, sixteen-year-old Sorcha thought she'd found her match in Rian, son of the late High King. The perfect choice. But crown princes don't marry overweight-magically-insignificant childhood friends. When I hit majority at twenty and was eligible for binding, I'd realized that. Crown princes marry willowy beauties, with magic and power to spare. I'd turned to Sam, the complete opposite of Rian, during that first Beltane when Rian snubbed me. But Sam turned out to be a dud; we dissolved our bond immediately after Lughnasadh the following year. Then came the next Beltane, and the cycle repeated. Noel was wild, the opposite of Sam, with raven-black hair begging to be touched, who looked *too* similar to Rian for me to claim I hadn't chosen him because of it. But our fling fizzled into nothingness; he wasn't Rian, and I couldn't make him be.

Jackson was next—not by choice but by elder decree. With two failures behind me, the elders no longer allowed me the freedom to choose. And Jackson was... Jackson was mean, creating scars

I'm still dealing with. By the time I'd finally been able to unbind from him, I felt like a shell of myself. And then there was Elliot, another choice of the elders. He could have been wonderful had I not still been mending from Jackson's cruelty. By the end of our time together, even Elliot had soured.

And I couldn't do it again. I couldn't bind to someone not my choice. I couldn't have my freedom, one of the only things that is truly mine—freedom and my cottage—taken from me simply because tradition demands it.

If I were Rian or any of the powerful fae heirs—those whose families own significant property in the civilized section of Avalaruin—I'd get extra time. No one expects Rian to bind to a wife after his first few seasons because once he does, he finally meets the requirements to take his crown. Unless those heirs call for a rule change and usurp the elder decree, but why bother? The elders give him and the other elite as much time as they want to sow their oats before settling down with a spouse.

But ordinary folk like us? We're essentially breeding stock, expected to perpetuate the fae lineage without complaint. If we refuse, we can no longer remain in Avalaruin. Although the fae aren't the only creatures that live here, we're all under the rule of the to-be High King and his elders. To be free, and not hide in the wilderness with those less-than-friendly creatures, I'd need to travel to the Aboveground, the world that lives upside down from ours, where the mages, werewolves, vampires, and humans have settled.

I'd always wanted to see the Aboveground as a child, but being forced to live there to avoid elder punishment—when it isn't my choice—isn't the same. Things might be lousy in Avalaruin, but it's still my home. My cottage is still the one where Mama and I dried herbs and created memories before she died. This is my life, pathetic though it may be. And this year is my last chance before permanent binding looms over me like an eternal sentence, taking me from my choices.

But I can't do it. I won't do it. I need my name off the betrothal list and then I can hide in my tiny cottage alone.

With the memories of all my past failures threatening to overwhelm me, I take a deep breath and—once I've blown the few curls that escaped my bun out of my face—begin to chant softly, my voice a whisper against the backdrop of the forest as dawn's first rays kiss the forest floor.

"By moon's soft light and shadow's veil, conceal my name, let truth not ail. From list and scroll, let it not be seen. Hide me well, by magic keen."

As I chant, I add the ingredients one by one to the bowl of water. First, the lavender, its fragrant buds floating on the surface. Next, the silver feather, which I dip into the water before laying it gently on top of the lavender in a cross. The obsidian comes next, sinking to the bottom and casting dark ripples through the liquid. Finally, I uncork the vial of my blood and let a few drops fall into the mixture, the red swirling and blending with the other elements, creating an eerie but beautiful effect.

As the charm combines, I can't help but think about Rian. If he were here, if we were as close as we used to be, he could remove my name from the betrothal lists with nothing but a thought. He was a master of illusions and wishes, his magic far superior to mine. All you need to do is wish for something hard enough and Rian is there to grant it. Usually.

He used to, at least.

But he's likely off with Isabel. They have never been considered being bound on Beltane, but everyone expects it. Isabel's mother owns half the free country, making it a strategic match. The elders will likely push for the binding in the next few years. Especially since the vampires just crowned a new queen. The elders won't want any talk of allying with other creatures through marriage, too traditional for that. Meaning Rian needs to be unavailable by the time the Vampire Queen comes looking.

The Vampire Queen should be so lucky. Isabel too. Fates, I'd give anything to bind to Rian. But I'm a realist. Hence, the enchantment, my last hope at avoiding a forced marriage to someone not of my choosing. If my name is off the list, there's nothing to bind.

I continue my chant, my voice growing stronger with each repetition as the sun begins to rise. "Obsidian's guard, and feather's flight, shield me now from betrothal sight. With blood as bond, this charm I cast, let my name fade, unseen, and pass."

The mixture begins to glow softly, a faint silver light emanating from the bowl. I want to squeal at my success. I've done it. I'm not the failure I believe myself to be.

But all too soon, something goes wrong. The lavender falls to the bottom of the bowl, the feather following. The blood looks to be congealing.

"No," I say, reaching for the items, my shoulders falling. "No, no no no. Come on!"

Panicked thoughts race through my mind as I try to salvage the spell, but it's too late. The sun has risen. Beltane has officially begun, meaning my name will remain on the list. I have three months to either find a partner on my own (hah!), vanish into the Aboveground and never return to Avalaruin... or face an immortal lifetime bound to a husband not of my choosing.

My heart sinks as I reach up to run my fingers through my wild brown hair, which became further unbound during my unsuccessful attempt at freeing myself, only to find that my arm feels unnaturally heavy.

Looking down, I see a thick golden cuff encircling my wrist, its shimmering surface betraying the magic imbued within it. A thin golden chain travels from my wrist to another wide cuff, one attached to another hand.

It's a handsome hand, if hands can be handsome (and they absolutely can). It has long-boned fingers that almost seem to spark with azure wish magic. There's a thin scar circling the tip of the index finger from when we'd dared each other to stick a finger into the mouth of a spark-frog. I have the same scar on my other, uncuffed, hand. Heart pounding, my gaze travels up that so-familiar hand, towards a golden skinned wrist with thick, strong veins, up a muscular arm and shoulder covered in black strands of hair, wild like an electrical storm. The tanned face smirking at me is sharp and angular, with high cheekbones and a strong jawline, angles I could draw in my sleep.

And then our eyes meet, his piercing ice-blue gaze meeting mine with amusement.

"Hello, love," Rian says from his seat beside me, lifting his wrist to make it clear that his hand is the one I am attached to. "Care to explain this wish?"

I WAS EIGHT YEARS old.

The sun was high in the sky, but still I felt cold as I sat alone in the meadow behind the forest that separates Mama's house from the rest of the community. We rented the tiny cottage from a neighbor, paying in tinctures until she finally bought the small plot just before she died.

It was the two of us against the world for the longest time. She kept me at home with her, trying to teach me magic herself, to avoid falling behind the other fae my age. It didn't stop the teasing though. But my lacking magical prowess wasn't the only thing kids liked to make fun of. Not knowing my father, being twice the size (horizontally, not vertically) of the other girls, they could take their pick.

That day, the other children who played in that meadow had long since left, their laughter and chatter fading into the distance. I stared at the grass, my fingers absently twisting a strand, tears prickling at the corners of my eyes. I had tried so hard to get the charm right, something Mama taught me the week before, but once again, it had fizzled out in a puff of smoke.

"I wish I had a friend," I whispered to the ground. "Someone who wouldn't laugh at me."

As if summoned by my wish, and I later learned that was exactly what had happened, a boy appeared at the edge of the meadow. He had tousled dark hair and ice-blue eyes that seemed to twinkle with a secret. He was a little taller than me, with an air of confidence that told me, even then, he always got what he wanted.

"Hi," he said, walking towards me with a crooked smile. "I'm Rian."

I wiped at my eyes, hoping my nose wasn't as red as a tomato, scraping my bushy curls away from my face. "Hi... I'm Sorcha."

"I heard you wished for a friend," Rian said, sitting down beside me.

"You heard me?"

"I have wish magic," he said, plucking at a strand of grass. "Sometimes, I can hear people's wishes.

Yours was very strong. You must've really meant it."

Mama hadn't told me much of the other kinds of magic. I knew they existed, of course. I think she thought I should focus on bettering my magic than getting caught up in something I didn't have. But she never mentioned wishcraft; it wasn't until Rian and I became friends that I realized how rare it was.

"And you came to... what?" I narrowed my eyes suspiciously. "Laugh at me too?"

"No," he said, grabbing another few strands of grass and plaiting them. "Isabel and Reggie were being boring. And since I heard your wish, I thought I could come and grant it." He leaned in close, and I felt compelled to do the same. "Don't tell my mom, though. She keeps saying wish magic is dangerous."

"I won't tell her," I promised. After all, I didn't know who she—or Rian—was until a year later.

With a flourish, he revealed what he'd been braiding out of grass. "Look, a crown!"

It was, in fact, a crown, one large enough to fit over my curly hair and embedded with sparkling daisies. Besides Mama's charms, it was the best piece of magic I'd seen in my young life.

"I have illusion magic too," he explained, handing it to me with a grin. "That's why it's bigger now. You should wear it!"

I looked down at the crown, somewhat shy. "I... I keep messing up my charms. And no one wants to play with me."

Rian tilted his head. "I can help you, if you'd like."

My heart lifted at the offer. "You'd do that?"

"Of course," Rian said with a grin. "What are friends for?"

I smiled, the first genuine smile I'd felt all day. "Thank you, Rian." I shoved the crown on my head.

We spent the next hours playing together, running through the meadow and trying out simple charms. He showed me a trick to make the flowers glow brighter, his illusion magic intertwining with my light charms, the only enchantment that ever worked for me. As we played, I laughed more than I had in a long time.

After a while, Rian glanced at the horizon, where the sun was sinking lower. "I should probably get back to my friends soon. But I had fun today, Sorcha. Can we play again tomorrow?"

My face fell a little at the thought of him leaving, but still I nodded. "I'd like that. Thank you for being my friend, Rian."

Rian smiled warmly and I swear I felt it like a blanket wrapping around me. "You're welcome, Sorcha. And remember, you're not alone. Whenever you need a friend, just make a wish."

"Undo it, Rian." My pale face is surely bloodless now. "Undo it right now."

As a young girl in love, I'd likened Rian to a sculpture carved from thunder and lightning, wrapped in the sinewy strength of a wild ocean wave, uncontrollable and able to drag you into the depths with him. I'd wanted to be overcome by him then. As an adult who had her heart broken, he looks like a different kind of danger, a predator whose beauty and colors are a warning of the poison within.

Rian smirks at me, resting his elbow on his knee and leaning against his cuffed hand. "In due time, dearest. But I find myself absolutely *thrilled* to discover what you were attempting to do."

My stomach twists as I consider how much I need to reveal before he'll take the damn cuffs off. "Today's Beltane," I begin cautiously.

A laugh bursts out of him, his gaze softening. "And this is how you find your next husband?" He gives me an indulgent smile. "Darling, if you wanted to bind to me, you could have simply asked instead of cuffing me together until Lughnasadh." He looks down at the cuff, turning it in the morning light. "Although, I'm honestly surprised none of the other eligible ladies have attempted this."

"You think *this* was my intention?" I gesture towards our chained hands, but the metal restricts my movements. My embarrassment and frustration start to boil over even as my body trembles from the morning chill.

"Obviously," he drawls. He traces a finger along the intricate design of the cuffs, the magic pulsating beneath his touch. "Otherwise, I would not be chained to your lovely self."

"I was trying to keep myself off the betrothal lists! To stop from being bound!" I snap, the sting of tears telling me how close I am to weeping. But I hadn't cried in front of anyone—except Rian—in years. And he didn't deserve my vulnerabilities.

"Oh, love," Rian sighs, pulling me into his embrace. It's a familiar gesture, but one that hasn't happened since I was eighteen, when he last rejected my advances.

Even so, the sudden touch sends a spark of heat down my spine, awakening a whirlwind of conflicting emotions within me.

"Were they that bad?" he asks softly. "Your bindings? You seemed happy for a time."

I take a deep breath, steadying myself before meeting Rian's intense gaze. His eyes, usually so full of mischief and warmth, now hold a hint of concern that makes my heart clench in my chest. But I won't admit those failures. "This is my last one, Rian," I whisper.

He runs his hands from my back to hooking over my plump hips, making my pulse quicken. "I'm aware," he says just as quietly. "Is there *no one* you could imagine binding to? No one you'd wi-want to?"

No one who would want me, I think bitterly. But I avoid the question and instead gesture towards the bowl and remnants of my failed charm. "I didn't wish for this, I promise," I tell him, wanting, irritatingly, to bury my face in the collar of his tunic and hide. I'd wished to bind to him at Lughnasadh, not be handcuffed to him. And I hadn't even truly done that.

"Mmhm," he hums. "Perhaps not in one straightforward wish, but it all came together in the end." He brushes a stray strand of hair behind my ear, only for it to fall back into my face. "You desired a connection of some kind, did you not?"

Hells, I'd give anything if I could bind to Rian, I remember thinking mid-chant. I keep my gaze focused on his shirt, staring at the strong jut of his collarbones through the fabric.

But he doesn't wait for my answer. "And you thought of me. As one does."

Self-preservation forces me to downplay my feelings. "I was thinking about how lucky you are to not be bound by these rituals," I explain. "You get to choose who you want."

His blue eyes darken. "Well, not everyone can be as lucky as I am," he says with a leer, one that doesn't appear as sincere as usual.

Are he and Isabel having difficulties? The thought fills me with an inappropriate sense of glee, but I quickly tamp it down. *Don't get sucked back into that maelstrom,* I tell myself. *You'll drown.*

"You could have ignored it," I remind him, somewhat petulantly. He does that enough. "Why grant this one?"

He tightens his grip on my hips, his eyes focused on the remains of my ritual space. "I didn't hear it all, simply your voice and a deep desire for something. I never expected to be handcuffed to your charming self."

"What did you think?" I ask, still petulant, even though his explanation makes sense. It's so much easier to blame him, after all.

His gaze shifts from me back to the cuffs in the span of a heartbeat. "A connection or some...thing. But enough about that, dearest. Let's figure out all the fun we're going to have with these things."

"You need to undo it," I say firmly.

He chuckles softly, the sound deep and rich. His eyes hold a teasing glint, as if he's thoroughly enjoying my predicament. "Shan't."

"Rian!" I shove him away, creating much-needed distance between us. It's my lacking strength, not the four-foot chain, that keeps him still overly close to me.

"Apologies, I should have said can't," he corrects himself with a mischievous smirk. "I can't remove it. Not until the wish is fulfilled."

"It's fulfilled!" My voice rises in desperation. "We're bound. That's it. There's nothing else."

The wish can't... expect me to bind to him at Lughnasadh, could it? That would kill me. Literally, as I'm sure the elders would murder me for jumping above my station, with no votes to support me. None of the enchantment guild would stand behind my apparent apathy for procedure.

I'm supposed to *accept* the elder's decree, not attempt to snag the crown.

He sighs dramatically, his hand reaching out to caress my cheek with a tenderness that belies his playful demeanor. "Apparently not. There must be something else to do to fulfill it. Remind me of the exact words?"

If he's forgotten, I'm not reminding him. I'd like to keep a little dignity for myself.

"I'll unwish it, then," I answer instead, clamping my eyes shut and concentrating fiercely. *Get these damn cuffs off me.*

When my eyes reopen, we both swivel our heads towards our bound hands, but the cuffs remain stubbornly locked in place.

"What's said is said, dearest," Rian chides gently. "You can't simply undo a wish. How would that work?"

It should work, I think mutinously. But magic is based on intent, and subconsciously, I probably prefer being bound to Rian than being alone.

"You could have ignored it," I repeat, frowning at him.

He tilts his head, studying me intently. "I don't ignore wishes."

My glare intensifies until his golden cheeks flush with what must be memories of the times he had *indeed* ignored my wishes.

"Then we figure out how to undo it," I declare. No way was I spending my final binding season literally chained to the one man who remains just out of reach. No one deserves that kind of pain.

Chapter 2

THE CUFF BITES INTO my wrist as I pull Rian through the labyrinthine corridors of his castle, the clinking of our involuntary bond punctuating every step with a reminder of the absurdity of our situation. I'd tried to undo it in the forest, cobbling together a half dozen enchantments, but either they didn't work, or my magic didn't. It's a toss-up. If only my light magic could have heated enough to melt the chains.

With no other options, I must turn to books, and find some other magic to remove the cuffs, the knowledge likely found in the former High King's library. We take the long route through the castle, sneaking through hidden passageways and back hallways to avoid being seen by any of his servants or staff. The front doors also hold dozens of wards against entrance, and I can't handle waiting for another fae to undo them to give me permission to enter. The last thing I want is for anyone else to see me in this situation: chained, desperate, and presumably clinging to scraps of hope.

As we scurry through the halls, I steal glances at Rian when he's not looking. It's been... years... since we spent any time together. At least since... Sam, perhaps. Certainly, I saw him; he is the future leader of our species, but we haven't spent time together since my first Beltane, when I finally, officially, gave up.

My eyes soak him in. The way his black cloak billows behind him as we walk, revealing glimpses of a well-fitted suit underneath, how the curve of his chiseled jawline is illuminated by the sconces—it all serves as a painful reminder of this cruel joke my subconscious has played on me. But now, it feels like some cruel trick, dredging up old memories of us, of a time when I trusted him, of a time when I trusted the world enough to have what I wanted.

Nearly sulking, I drag him down a hallway towards his bedroom, only two turns away from the private entrance to the library.

"Sorcha, if you want to spend time in my bedroom, all you have to do is ask," Rian quips, stumbling slightly as he tries to match my pace, his voice laced with that infuriatingly charming humor.

"We're going to the library," I snap back, not daring to meet his gaze for fear of him seeing how much that thought intrigues me. I haven't been in his bedroom since I was fifteen, when my mom died, and I couldn't handle being alone.

We dash past his bedroom door, and I force myself not to think about how many other women have visited that space over the years. Isabel probably has her own toothbrush and a designated side of the bed. The thought stings more than it should.

Finally, the doors to the library loom before us, ancient wood carved with depictions of long-forgotten legends, and we step into the High King's sanctuary of knowledge. The vastness of the space envelops us immediately, the cavernous room stretching upwards into shadowy heights where books seem to defy gravity, perched on shelves that look to be floating in midair. The wooden floors are polished to perfection, reflecting the light and making the room seem even larger. Dust motes dance in the slants of light that pierce the library's solemn dimness from the high windows, giving it an ethereal quality. As I breathe in the musty air of the library, I can almost taste the pages of ancient books on my tongue. There's a bitterness to it, but it reminds me of the countless hours I spent here with Rian when we were young.

"Behold, the repository of ages," Rian murmurs, his tone dripping with sarcasm.

"I've been here before," I remind him.

His gaze sweeps over the endless rows of books before landing back on me. "I recall. You used to come daily for a time. Before you outgrew my games and instead took advantage of my generosity towards these books."

"Just because I could read a book a day and you couldn't, that doesn't mean I took—"

His voice drops low as he interrupts me. "Are you sure I cannot tempt you into my bedroom?" My eyes are likely as wide as saucers, but he continues before I can react further. "You'll be surprised to learn I have my very own book collection now. Isabel convinced me. There are a few on a certain *intimate* kind of magic only practiced with a partner."

At this explanation, at the mention of Isabel, my heart rate slows, and I offer him a strained smile. "This isn't a pleasure trip, Rian." I hold up our cuffed hand before he interrupts to make some suggestive comment about 'pleasure.' "We're looking for books to uncuff us."

He pouts theatrically and leans against a shelf dedicated to fae magic. "I know, dearest. But surely some of my books might be helpful."

"Do you have any on wishcraft in your bedroom?" I ask, raising a skeptical eyebrow.

He taps a finger against his plush lips in thought. My gaze follows that finger until I mentally force my focus elsewhere. Just because this is the closest Rian and I have been together—and for such an extended period—in years, it doesn't mean I let myself get distracted by his handsome face. We need to get unbound. In less than a week, I'll be forced into the first courtship outing and I can't have the crowned prince cuffed to me. If I must lose all my freedoms, at least let me do it on *my* terms. Not the laughingstock of society.

"No," he says, his voice a deep rumble that reverberates through the library.

I blink in surprise, having the horrible thought that his magic somehow includes mind reading, before I remember I'd asked him a question.

"Anything on wishcraft would have remained here. Alas," he finishes, his gaze sweeping over the towering shelves of books with disinterest.

"Then this is where we'll remain."

"But in my bedroom, I can bask in my life lacking in responsibilities while you go rabid over the books I do have without subjecting me to all this dust." His nostrils twitch as he speaks, clearly not pleased with the idea of spending any more time in the library.

"You can bask in here just as easily as there," I tell him, rolling my eyes at his theatrics. My fingers trace the ridges of leather-bound spines as I scan the shelves, searching for any book that could hold information on wish magic. Every book I withdraw from its resting place releases a puff of age, revealing that when I stopped coming to the library, so must have Rian and anyone else who might have been interested.

"Ah, 'The Lamentations of Ancient Queens.' Sounds... cheerful," Rian drawls from beside me, his voice a melody of feigned interest. "I should read that one. Wouldn't want you to repeat it."

"Focus, Rian," I chide without looking up from the volume in my hands. The script in my hands is an archaic scrawl, almost indecipherable, but I force patience into my heart. Except with each frustrated flip through antiquated texts, my desperation mounts. "We need to find *something* on wishcraft."

"You know as well as I do that we hold no such books here. Father destroyed them all," he replies, absently running a hand through his tousled hair, the golden cuff on his wrist catching the light.

"After your mother died." I remember now, bitterness and loss tinging my words. His mother, the High Queen, had passed away a year after mine.

We had found solace in each other's company during my grief over Mama, but he'd started pulling away when his mother passed. Pushing aside the painful memories, I continue, "And with you as the only remaining wish practitioner..."

"We are indeed in a bind," he finishes for me, his tone lighter than the word warrants.

I close my eyes tight, letting the disappointment wash off me, before marching us to the books on mortal books. As he must, Rian trails after me.

"You could have told me that to begin with," I grumble.

"I assumed you read between the lines of what'd I'd said," he drawls. He raises an eyebrow. "Did you hear that? I made a pun. Twice over, now."

I stomp my way towards the section on thought magic, hoping it might be a brother to wishcraft and get us out of this mess. "I don't know why you're not taking this seriously," I tell him. "You're stuck with me too."

"Why should that bother me?" he says, flapping a hand as though it happens so often he's bored with it. With a snap of his free hand, the illusion of what looks to be a calendar unfurls in front of my face. "I have nothing scheduled for... weeks, really. And then it's another month before Litha and—"

I wave my hand, dispelling the calendar. "Great. With all your free time, you should be helping me unbind us."

"We could go to the elders now," he says, his voice low, testing.

My eyes snap to his, and there's a heat in his expression that warms my cheeks. "And admit I cuffed the prince?"

"And tell them of our... binding. If we're stuck together until Lughnasadh, it seems inevitable." He leans in, his breath fanning my hair.

I straighten. "Do you want them to kick me out of Avalaruin?"

"Of course not," he says, waving a negligent hand. "Nor would they."

My brows raise, wondering when he got so naïve. "Do you have the votes to keep me from trouble?"

You only need three votes to overturn a decision of the seven elders, a small number certainly, but difficult. Most people don't want to attack the tradition of the elders, it's the tradition that keeps the *rest* of Avalaruin from rebelling. No one wants to risk another fae war, one that brought all other creatures to heel. A handful, those that allied with the fae, were given their own realm in a newly created world upside down from ours. The High King—and his elders—rule absolute. And unless Rian takes his crown, the elders alone remain in charge.

I'm barely a member of my guild. I'm not even invited to the meetings. I'm certainly not talented enough to be worth standing up to the elders for. And while Rian is the only member of the wishcraft guild, most of the illusion guild—his other magic—work directly for the elders. Or are his elite friends, who likely revel in their privileges and have no need to help the peons below them.

Apparently, he hadn't considered that as he frowns, and I take the opportunity to drag him where I want him. We finally reach the shelves on mortal thought magic, and he scoffs.

"Darling, if all the knowledge of the fae can't help us, these mortal scribblings will likely do nothing. We should resign ourselves to our fate and start picking out our Samhain costumes now. I'm thinking constable and prisoner."

"We need to consider all possibilities," I retort, my grip tightening around a tome so ancient its title has worn away. "The fae may not have the answers, but there's lore here, Rian. Something could give us the answer."

He hums thoughtfully, a sound that seems to vibrate through the metal binding us together. I tug at the cuff that links us, a vain attempt to gain some semblance of autonomy as I reach for another volume. Rian saunters after me, his steps leisurely and out of sync with my own hurried pace.

"Ah, 'The Enchanted Epochs,'" he drawls, peering over my shoulder with feigned interest. "Does it speak of love potions, perhaps? Or maybe the secret to charming fair maidens like yourself?"

"Neither," I reply curtly, flipping through pages stained from either the passage of time or some kind of alcohol.

"Come now, Sorcha," he chides, leaning closer so his breath tickles my ear. "You can't expect me to believe all this fervor is solely for our little… predicament."

My cheeks warm at his proximity, an involuntary response. The heat emanates from his body, the closeness a constant reminder of the chain that binds us—a chain forged by my ill-fated wish and *apparently* too-eager and too-sentimental heart.

"Focus, Rian," I implore, though my words lack conviction. Ten years ago, I would have reveled in the attention, soaked in the light of his playful eyes. Ten years ago, I would have thought it was real. But life, and time, and *Rian*, showed me the error in my ways.

"Always," he replies with a sly smile. "On everything but the task at hand."

I sigh, my resolve wavering like a flame in the wind. It is true, my feelings for Rian have always lingered just beneath the surface, an undercurrent to every interaction. Yet, here in the musty silence of the library, the weight of my unrequited affection bears down upon me with renewed gravity.

"Must you make light of everything?" I ask, trying to keep the hurt from seeping into my voice.

"Only because you make heavy of everything else," he retorts, his grin faltering as he catches the edge in my tone.

"Maybe one of us needs to," I mutter. After all, the person who will be negatively affected by this connection won't be Rian. He'll laugh it off, a careless wish gone wrong, one he somehow felt obligated to grant. I'll be the butt of the joke, the woman with four broken bindings behind her, who tried to steal the crowned prince and couldn't even manage that correctly.

Likely *Isabel* would have made the wish count, made it a real binding, not simply magical handcuffs.

He surveys me then, his expression softening, as if sensing my inner turmoil that churns like a stormy sea. For a moment, the teasing guise falls away, and something akin to understanding flickers in his eyes.

"Sorcha," he begins, reaching out with his free hand, but I pull away before he can touch me, afraid that comfort might shatter my resolve.

"Let's just find out how to end the wish," I say, steeling myself against the pull of his gaze.

"Of course," Rian concedes, but there is a new-found gentleness to his voice. "Although I hate to take myself from your presence so soon, we could consult the fomorian witches? I've been meaning to visit, check for any fomenting revolution. We could—"

"It wouldn't work," I cut him off, closing another book with a soft thud. "They're more likely to saw our hands off instead." The wild things, those dark anti-fae that consort with creatures of nightmares, they live in the surrounding forests, brought to heel through the Great War and remain resentful of it. They'd slit your throat and force you to thank them for the pleasure.

"Then we're searching for a needle in a haystack," Rian murmurs, though his gaze has turned thoughtful, watching me with an intensity that makes my heart flutter against my will. "Except the needle might just be a figment of your hopeful imagination."

My eyes meet his, his pupils as dark and fathomless as the depths of the Unseen Lake. For an instant, the vast library seems to shrink around us, the walls pressing close with the gravity of our plight. "Hope isn't real," I say softly, turning back to the endless rows of knowledge. "I can't rely on something as inconstant as hope."

I reach for another aged volume, the heavy book releasing a cloud of dust as I heft it onto the reading table, the golden cuffs clinking in protest at the sudden movement. Rian watches silently now, his earlier frivolity replaced by a pensiveness that strangely suits him. Perhaps this is a glimpse of him as High King, when he takes a bride. For a fleeting minute, I wonder what thoughts wander through his mind, but the urgency of our situation leaves no time for me to enjoy his proximity.

We sit together, bound by metal and uncertainty, as shadows lengthen across the library's stone floors. The only sound is the soft rustle of ancient pages and the steady rhythm of two hearts caught in an enchanted snare.

"Sorcha," Rian drawls, breaking the quiet with his mirth-laced tone. Apparently, his solemnity doesn't last through dinnertime. "You realize that we've been in this dusty tomb for hours? Even my charm has its limits."

"Your 'charm'?" I can't help but let a smile tug at the corner of my lips. Apparently, *my* solemnity needs a break too. "I wasn't aware you had any."

"Ah, you wound me," he feigns a dramatic gasp, placing a hand over his heart. The movement brings his arm against mine, the cold metal of our cuffs a stark reminder of our predicament.

"I only have a few more books to go. If we're lucky, I'll find the one to break this curse and then you can go enjoy your evening." My voice is stern, but inside, my heart flutters traitorously. I hate how, even in the direst of times, his closeness sets my nerves alight.

"Curse?" He chuckles, leaning in so close that his nose nearly brushes against my cheek. "I'd call it an unexpected partnership."

"Partnership implies cooperation," I retort, trying to ignore the warmth radiating from his body. "You're hardly cooperating."

"But am I not here assisting you in your quest for freedom?" His eyes sparkle with mischief, yet behind the playful façade, I sense an undercurrent of something else—something unreadable and deep.

"By making light of everything and slowing me down?" I sigh, turning back to the book, my fingers tracing the leather-bound cover etched with cryptic symbols that dance under the flickering light of my will-o'-the-wisp.

"Laughter is the light in the darkness, Sorcha. And right now, you could use a little light." His voice softens, and for a moment, the fool's mask slips, revealing the thoughtful man beneath, the man I once thought I knew.

"That's the only magic I can do, Rian," I murmur. "I don't need light. I need freedom. This is my last chance, Rian. With my charm failing and my name still on the list, this is my only opportunity for it. It's fix this or leave Avalaruin. And I can't bind to someone while handcuffed to you."

"I will not let you waste this chance," he says with a surprising gentleness, his hand brushing mine as he helps turn a page, sending a jolt up my arm. "Although I don't find the thought of being cuffed to you forever all that difficult."

My mind reels at the thought. "It would make for an uncomfortable binding ceremony," I murmur, half to myself. I can imagine it now: we don't find a solution, I can't leave Avalaruin, the elders won't let me bind to Rian, of course, so Rian stands behind me, making silly faces at whatever fae I get bound to. Then in another few years, I stand behind him, sullen and chained, as he binds to Isabel. I refuse to even consider any of the practicalities: dressing, cleaning, or... bed sport.

"Would that be so terrible? Being bound to me?" His question hangs in the air, laced with an emotion I can't place.

"Your future Queen might take issue with it," I reply quickly, too quickly, my heart betraying my words with its erratic drumming.

He leans in. "Perhaps she doesn't yet understand the fun handcuffs can be."

I clear my throat. "Fun?" My voice wavers as I glance up at him, finding a mischievous glint in his eyes. His proximity is intoxicating, the warmth of his breath on my cheek and his teasing innuendos a dangerous game of temptation. But beneath the playful banter, there's a flicker of something more, something that ignites a spark of longing buried deep within me. One I doused with ice years ago.

The library around us fades into insignificance, the musty scent of old parchment mixing with the heady aroma of his presence. The weight of his gaze is heavy, as tangible as the shackles binding us together, and yet there's a softness in his expression that contradicts his usual cavalier demeanor.

Rian leans closer, his breath warm against my ear as he murmurs, "There are different ways to interpret this binding, you know." His voice low, intimate. "Perhaps we've been looking at this from the wrong angle all along."

I swallow hard, trying to ignore the way my heart races at his words. "What do you mean?"

A slow smile curls at the corners of his lips, a faint dimple appearing on one cheek as he studies my reaction. His touch lingers on the edge of my hand, his thumb tracing a gentle pattern that sends sparks dancing along my skin.

"Perhaps this is our opportunity to... engage each other. The way we never did in years past."

This is classic Rian, turning everything into a game, weaving his charm around me like a net. But I won't let myself be caught again. Not this time.

I tear my gaze away, back towards the book in my lap, before I feel compelled to stare back up at his bright eyes. "This is no time for games, Rian," I say, my tone firmer than I feel inside. He had some many chances, I gave him so many opportunities, and only now, when we have no future to speak of, when mine is in the balance, does he decide I'm worth a romp or two?

His hand lingers on mine as he leans back, the intensity in his eyes not wavering. "Games imply a winner and loser. My suggestion would leave us both quite satisfied." His voice is a whisper, laden with an unexpected sincerity that has no place in this sensual proposition.

As much as his proximity sets my heart racing and my pulse quickening, I can't afford to lose myself in the tantalizing dance of what-ifs and maybes. Rian will marry Isabel soon and give Avalaruin the High Queen it's been waiting for. And now I'm destined to marry some awful bear and have a lackluster life until I inevitably shuffle off from boredom or sadness. Letting myself experience him, letting my heart get broken anew isn't on the agenda.

I draw back, breaking the spell of his nearness with a steadying breath. "We need to keep looking."

Rian's expression flickers, a shadow passing over his features. "Of course, dearest. Do finish your reading. I won't distract you anymore, Sorcha. I promise."

With a deep inhale, I turn to the last book on mortal magic the library offers. My fingers trace the embossed title, 'Arcana of the Post-Mortal Ages,' before flipping the book open.

The pages crackle as I turn them, the scent of old parchment a familiar comfort to my anxious heart. Then, amidst human spells of summoning and banishing, I find it—a passage about the Oracle of Shadows. It is said to be a being of great power, living in an ancient crypt nestled within the vampire enclave Aboveground. It knows all that was and will be.

"Look at this, Rian." I point at the exquisite drawings that flank the text—vague, shadowy figures standing sentinel around an indistinct form. "The Oracle might be our answer."

"An oracle, you say?" He leans closer, his breath tickling my ear again. "Do they deal in wish magic?"

My gaze returns to the page, hungry for every detail. "It doesn't say, but they 'know all.'" I look back at him, hope slowly rising. "They should know how to *break* the wish. It's worth a try, isn't it?"

"Agreed." His smile returns, but it doesn't quite reach his eyes. Likely because our time in the library has just increased.

I return to the book. With each word I devour, the room seems to fade away until nothing exists but the lore of the Oracle. Its keeper is a mystery, its purpose enigmatic, yet the possibility that it could explain how to sever the magical bond between us is too tantalizing to ignore.

Finally, after minutes that feel like eternities, I close the book with a soft thud, the sound echoing throughout the cavernous space. My fingers linger on the cover, caressing the leather-bound tome as if it is a lifeline. In a way, it is—the only key I've found to unlocking the cuffs.

"Darling?" Rian's voice is barely audible, a ghostly murmur in the vastness of the library.

I look at him, caught in the silver of his gaze, the world tilting. "We should seek the Oracle in the Oiche," I say. And once I'm uncuffed, I can decide whether I want to remain there as a free woman or return and let the elders choose my future.

"Then we shall," he agrees, standing tall beside me. "I'd follow wherever you lead."

"You have to," I tell him, my words a brittle shield against the tumult inside.

He smiles, something that looks full of secrets. "Just so."

Chapter 3

We plan to leave immediately. The quicker, the better. Rian quibbles, claiming he needs to remain for one reason or another, even inviting me to a string of dinners, but one look at my scowl shuts that down. He had shown me an empty calendar after all; lies about social events wouldn't sway me.

After my suggestion to return to my cottage to fetch proper traveling clothes, he stops short, giving me a look that borders on amused disbelief.

"No need," he says with a flick of his wrist. In an instant, the air around me shimmers, a soft magic sweeping over my body. A warm, prickling sensation ripples over my skin, and I glance down in time to watch my plain apothecary garb transform into fitted leather trousers and a tunic of deep forest green, perfectly suited for slipping through shadows and wandering unknown roads. It's his illusion magic at work, but it's the first time he's put it to practical use on me since childhood.

"Don't thank me all at once," he teases, a mischievous glint in his eye.

I bristle, tugging at the unfamiliar fabric. "Thank you? It's the least you can do." Better I think that than feel as though I owe him.

He slips a sword into a scabbard at his waist, a quick, fluid movement that reminds me how accustomed he is to carrying such a weapon, and hands me a dagger. "I suppose. Although, if it were truly my choice, I'd have given you something... a little more revealing."

I roll my eyes as I take the dagger, knowing it's more for decoration than protection. "Be sure to leave a note explaining your absence to Isabel," I say pointedly.

He just smirks at me.

A few minutes later, we slip from the castle, the exterior walls tinted in the deep shades of violet at dusk. Rian's earlier quip about his "life lacking responsibilities" rings true; not a soul bothers us as we make our way back through those abandoned hallways. The stillness only adds to my unease, reminding me that the castle is his world, his life—and I'm a trespasser in it.

Then, we head toward the Unseen Lake, where the portal to the Aboveground is hidden. The Unseen Lake is a body of water untouched by light, where not even the sharpest eye can penetrate its depths. We used to visit when we were children, all young ones did, to dare each other to cross the rickety bridge to Tixia Island at the center of the water. Rian and I played there when we were just kids, dreaming of the world beyond Avalaruin. But perilous creatures, like the finfolk, kelpies, seawolves, and more, are found within the depths.

The path from the capital, where the castle is, to the wilds of Avalaruin is long, winding through murky swamps and spindly trees that seem to whisper secrets of their own. Any number of creatures could have come upon us, but even without taking his crown, Rian is powerful. He leads the way with a confident stride, his arm looped through mine, for necessity—the damn cuffs—and safety, to keep me from tripping in the dark.

As we near the Lake's edge hours later, an unsettling chill sweeps over me, the kind of cold that slips beneath your skin and sticks in your bones. The waters lap gently against the shore, but the sound seems oddly muted, as though absorbed by the omnipresent gloom. I blink and it feels as though dozens of eyes in the water blink in response.

"You aren't afraid, are you, dearest?" Rian asks, his hand briefly touching my back to steer me along the wooden bridge.

"I'm not afraid," I reply. "I've just... never left Avalaruin, you know that."

"How lucky that I can experience this with you," he says.

I frown at him. "I'd rather it be under different circumstances," I mutter to myself. Like by my choice. Or even when I'm *fleeing* Avalaruin.

"Me as well," Rian says.

I search his expression for insincerity, but find none. I try not to let it mean something, but my heart doesn't want to behave.

The bridge creaks beneath our weight as we make our way towards Tixia Island, the dark waters of the Unseen Lake swirling ominously below. Rian walks beside me, his presence a constant reassurance and a lingering temptation that I know I can't succumb to.

As we reach the middle of the bridge, a sudden gust of wind howls through the trees, causing the bridge to sway precariously. I grasp onto Rian's arm tightly, my heart pounding in my chest. His laughter rings out as he steadies me with a firm grip.

"Don't worry," he says with a mischievous twinkle in his eye. "I won't let anything happen to you."

We step onto Tixia Island, the ground solid beneath my feet after the shaky bridge. The peaks of the island loom before us, an indistinct mass shrouded in mist. Somewhere on that island lies the cave—the passage that will lead us to the Aboveground, to light and air and a world vastly different from the one I've always known. The place Rian and I planned to visit when we grew up, before life showed me that things didn't always work out. The place I might have to abscond to if I don't get these cuffs figured out and stop myself from binding on Lughnasadh.

"There it is." Rian stops abruptly, pointing toward a jagged outline barely discernible against the backdrop of night.

I quickly charm up a will-o'-the-wisp, a small blue faelight that sits on my shoulder as we stumble towards the cave. The entrance yawns wide before us, a gaping maw that seemed to swallow the feeble glow of my light. Stepping through the mouth of the cave, Rian's hand grazes mine, an electric jolt that sends heat cascading down my spine. His touch lingers just a second too long, leaving a trail of that warmth across my skin.

I shift away, focusing instead on the serpentine shadows dancing along the jagged walls. The cave seems to breathe around us, its exhales stirring up ancient dust and secrets. Rian leads us, his movements confident yet unnervingly careful.

"Watch your step," he murmurs, reaching out to steady me as my foot slips on an unseen stone. His arm encircles my waist, holding me close for an instant that stretches out before he releases me, leaving an imprint on my senses.

"Thank you," I manage, my voice a whisper lost in the cavernous expanse. But gratitude isn't the only thing swelling within me—resentment simmers beneath the surface, resentment at the ease with which he unbalances me, not just physically but emotionally, always keeping me teetering on the edge of something more profound.

We navigate the cave's twists and turns, descending deeper into the belly of the earth. Then, without warning, the oppressive confines of Avalaruin give way to an expanse so vast, so unexpected, that I halt in my tracks.

"Wait until you see this," Rian says.

I was twenty years old.

The sun was dipping below the horizon as Rian and I strolled through the enchanted forest. We were walking away from Mama's cottage, the only one remaining in the woods, now with just a single occupant. Me.

The air was filled with the perfume of blossoming flowers and the subtle whir of magic, signaling the start of Beltane, a time of anticipation. But for me, it was also a reminder of the looming deadline: in three months, during Lughnasadh, I would have to find a partner for the binding ceremony.

I had wished and wished for this moment, when I was of majority, for Rian to see me as more than a friend, to finally acknowledge the love I had harbored for him since they were children. That hope dwindled when he'd denied me at his first Beltane. He'd looked at me, a fleeting glance that had set my heart racing; the way he had seemed about to say something important, only to be interrupted by Isabel. And when we'd finally spoken, he'd denied me again.

Hope may have dwindled after that rejection, but it still lingered within me, ready to grow at the slightest hint of attention from him.

Today was the first time we'd spoken in months. I wouldn't let his rejection choose my future; I would do that. So, I'd thrown myself into finding something else to fill my time, something other than the image of Rian's smile. I could never replace Mama as an herbalist, but I could at least keep the fields growing. So long as I didn't use magic. The last time I'd tried, I set the hellebore on fire.

Rian likely didn't notice the distance I put between us, simply popping in and out of my life at a whim as his own was a whirlwind of activity. But he'd arrived at my cottage today with a bright smile and a plea that I come with him. We were friends, I reminded myself, even if we're no longer close. And I let him drag me away.

"Wait until you see this," he said, leading me to a secluded glen nearby.

My jaw dropped as I took in the picturesque setting only steps away from my shabby abode.

The glen was transformed into a magical haven, with fairy lights twinkling like stars, a crystal-clear stream running through the center, and flowers of every color imaginable blooming in perfect harmony. A table was set up by the stream, covered with delicate lavender linens and an array of delicious treats.

"Rian, this is… incredible," I said, my voice filled with awe and longing. "It's the most beautiful thing I've ever seen."

His smile widened, his eyes softening as he looked at me. "I wanted to create something special. Something that would make anyone feel cherished."

My heart ached and ice pooled in my veins. Those feelings I'd buried still bring pain, even when I've done all I could go forget them. I couldn't lie to myself—I wanted more than anything for this setup to be mine, that Rian felt the same way about me as I did about him. At one point, there had been so many signs… But signs weren't surety. It was always Isabel.

"Isabel will love it," I said, voicing it out for him so he wouldn't have to twist the knife any further.

His brows furrowed slightly, but before he could respond, Isabel appeared, her eyes lighting up at the sight of Rian. She was, as usual, undeniably beautiful, with her long auburn hair cascading down her back in gentle waves and her deep green eyes reflecting the magic around her. Even her skin, an umber brown, appeared to glow in the golden light.

"Rian! This is amazing!" Isabel exclaimed, rushing towards him, and linking her arm through his. "I can't believe you did all this."

His attention shifts to Isabel, his smile still in place but now directed at someone else. I couldn't deny it anymore; my long-time suspicions were confirmed and there was nowhere for hope to take root.

At least I'd kept my heart somewhat protected, hiding it from the frustration and sorrow that always wanted to burn through me when I saw him. I knew Rian cared for me, but clearly not in the way I wanted. Perhaps he saw me as nothing more than a friend, a confidante. The realization cut deep, but I had to accept it. I couldn't keep living in a fantasy, hoping for something that might never come.

I made myself a vow then. I would no longer wait for Rian. I would no longer let herself be hurt by his unintentional neglect. I would choose something different, better, a companion that wanted me as much as I him. I turned away, unable to watch any longer. As I walked away from the beautiful scene, I almost bumped into Sam, a short fae with blond hair and deep brown eyes. He was the complete opposite of Rian in both looks and personality. *Perfect.*

"Sorcha, are you alright?" Sam asked, his fingers flexing against my arms where he'd caught me.

I took a deep breath, trying to steady my emotions. "I'm fine, Sam. Just... needed a moment."

He studied me for a moment, then nodded. "I understand. It's my first Beltane season, too."

I looked up at him, a sudden idea forming. "Sam, would you... would you accompany me on a courting date?"

He nearly gulped, but managed a shy smile. "I'd love to."

And I thought I felt the tiniest bit of warmth cracking the ice within.

I BLINK AGAINST THE memories and brightness, letting both fade away, but the ache in my chest remains. The reminder will be something to keep close on this emotionally fraught visit.

When the world around me reappears, I see what Rian wished to show me. We've emerged into a world awash with color and life—a stark contrast to the somber tones of the Unseen Lake and Tixia island we left behind. Tixia Island has been transformed into the vibrant Heriot Island, Unseen Lake into Prism Lake.

Here, in the Aboveground, the air is alive with the chorus of hidden creatures, the scent of wildflowers, and the caress of a breeze that whispers promises of freedom.

"Beautiful, isn't it?" Rian's voice breaks the spell, and I turn to find his gaze not on the landscape but on me. I look away, unsettled by the intensity in his eyes.

"Unlike anything I've ever seen," I reply honestly, instead drinking in the sight of rolling hills and sprawling forests that stretch to the horizon. The sun hangs low in the sky, making the leaves shimmer like emeralds set ablaze.

For a moment, we stand there, enveloped in the beauty of the Aboveground. In that suspended moment, I almost forget about the cuffs, and the ache in my heart that I don't want to acknowledge.

But reality crashes back in as Rian closes the distance between us with a single step.

"I've always wanted to take you here," he admits. His hand lifts, a lock of my hair captured between his fingers as he brushes it away from my face with a tenderness that sends shivers down my spine. There's sincerity in his eyes, or at least what appears to be sincerity, and my heart races with uncertainty.

A distant sound breaks through the moment—a soft melody carried on the wind and I press as far away as the cuffs will allow.

"Come on," he says, offering his hand with a smile that doesn't quite reach his eyes. "There's more to see."

Reluctantly, I place my hand in his, allowing him to lead me into this new world. After a short walk, the trail ends abruptly, as though the earth has decided to halt its own expansion, surrendering to the vastness of the Prism Lake. In the Aboveground, its crystal-clear waters reflect the surrounding trees and mountains, and reveal the smooth stones lining the bottom. The setting sun casts a golden glow over the water, making it look like a literal paradise.

A solitary boat bobs gently at the water's edge. My gaze lingers on the vessel, its dark wood etched with swirling patterns.

"Seems our ride is here," I murmur.

Rian moves ahead, his steps sure and swift. With a grace that belies his warrior's physique, he leaps aboard, then turns to offer his hand. I take it, the repeated touch igniting a flutter in my chest that I quickly smother beneath layers of resolve.

"Careful, Sorcha," he teases, his voice low and playful. "Wouldn't want you to fall in before we've even started."

I scoff, pulling away once safely aboard. "As if you'd let me." The words escape, laced with unintended meaning, and I busy myself with looking anywhere but at him. "Because you'd fall in too, because of the cuffs," I add quickly.

"I'd jump," he says.

The smile in his voice pulls my gaze upward, searching for any hint of the real Rian beneath the charming facade he wears like a second skin.

Is any of it genuine?

I turn away, letting my fingers trail over the intricately carved patterns on the boat's edge.

We set off, the oars magically cutting through the glassy surface with rhythmic precision. As we glide across the lake, the sun dips lower, its dying light casting a melancholy glow upon the waters.

It isn't long before ethereal voices rise from the depths, their melodies sweet and haunting. Rian's head turns subtly toward the sound, his eyes gleaming with a mixture of curiosity and mischief.

"The sirens," he says, a smirk playing on his lips. "Their songs are as dangerous as they are beautiful, meant to lure unwary travelers to a watery grave."

"Is that a warning for me or for yourself?" I ask, raising a brow.

He chuckles, leaning back with an ease that irks me. "For both of us, perhaps. But I find it hard to fear something so enchanting."

"Enchanting isn't the word I'd use," I retort, folding my arms as I watch him, the chain taut between us.

"Come now, Sorcha. Where's your sense of adventure? It's not every day one gets to converse with the neighbors."

The boat slices through the still waters. The sirens' voices weave a magnetic spell around us. Even with my eyes fixed upon the mist covering the distant shore, I can't shut out their call—a melody of longing, of desires whispered in the darkest hours.

As we pass through the heart of the siren territory, their forms rise from the water, their eyes gleaming with a mesmerizing light. I glance at Rian, expecting to see a flicker of caution in his eyes, but there's only fascination. The sirens' voices grow louder, their haunting songs weaving a spell around us, closing in on Rian and the attention he gives them.

"They're quite taken with you," I mutter, unable to keep the bitterness from seeping into my tone.

Rian chuckles, his gaze lingering on the sirens who flutter around our boat like exotic birds. "Can you blame them?"

Yes, I want to scream. *Yes, because you're toying with them just as you always toy with me.*

One of them, with hair a mix of seaweed and shining pearls and eyes like liquid silver, swims closer to Rian, her graceful movements hypnotic.

I watch, powerless, as he leans over the boat's edge, his hand skimming the water close enough for her fingers to brush his. The siren's eyes gleam with a predatory light, her lips curving in a knowing smile. As he continues to engage with the temptresses, their laughter mingling with his, an icy knot forms in my stomach. This is Rian—charming, reckless, and utterly untethered by the concerns that bind lesser men.

"Come join us in the depths, handsome traveler," she beckons, her voice a luring whisper that ignites a spark of possessiveness within me.

Before I can stop him, Rian leans forward, his hand outstretched toward the siren, touching her cheek just as he's so recently touched mine. "As tempting as your offer is, I have other matters to attend to."

I watch, a mix of relief and frustration swirling in my chest as Rian resists the siren's invitation. The boat glides forward, leaving the alluring creatures behind. The haunting melody fades into the distance.

Rian turns his gaze to me, a glimmer of mischief dancing in his eyes. "You were worried for a moment there, weren't you?"

The ache within tightens as I realize how easily he moves from one enchantment to the next, leaving broken fragments of longing in his wake. Rian lives in a world where everything is fleeting—a game of minutes, each one savored and then discarded. And in that realization, another pang of sadness blooms, knowing that whatever lies ahead, the journey will be filled with more personal demons than I ever anticipated.

I scoff, masking the turmoil beneath my calm facade. "Not in the slightest. It would have served you right to be pulled into their depths."

He laughs, a sound that mingled too easily with the siren's own beguiling laugh. "And what a way to go," he teases back, but his eyes never leave the sirens that grow smaller and smaller as we sail away from them.

I push aside the heartache churning within me, focusing instead on the looming silhouette of the vampire district in the distance. When the vampire capital of Fuil finally emerges from the mist, it's with an ominous beauty—spires rising like jagged teeth against the sky.

"Welcome to Oiche, the Court of Eternal Rest," Rian says grandly, extending his arm in a mock gesture of courtesy. "Ironic as inhabitants rarely receive any, given their immortal status."

"Is everything a joke to you?" I ask, my resentment simmering just beneath the surface.

"Sorcha," Rian says softly, reaching out to catch a strand of my hair that had slithered forward, "I—"

"Please, don't," I interrupt, stepping back from his touch. If he notices the tremor in my voice, he gives no sign. Each joke, each careless touch, is another reminder that I'm just a distraction until something more captivating comes along. "Let's just get on with it," I say curtly, leaping from the boat and striding ahead toward the looming gates, dragging him with me. Interacting with Rian was a dance I had grown weary of, my feet sore from the steps I never truly mastered. "The sooner we consult the Oracle, the sooner I can be free of this charade."

"You do know I wouldn't have left you in the boat, don't you." He phrases it like a question, but it isn't. "I would have taken you with me and we could have explored the depths of Prism Lake together," he adds.

"You'd have no choice but to take me," I remind him. "Because of the cuffs."

I can feel his gaze on me as we navigate through the cobblestone streets leading into the city. "Even without them, dearest," he says. "As we always planned to as children."

I quicken my pace, refusing to meet his gaze as the memories of our shared childhood adventures wash over me like a bittersweet wave. We had once dreamed of exploring the far reaches of Avalaruin together, daring to venture where few had trodden. But those dreams had crumbled beneath the weight of reality, leaving only fragments of what could have been.

"We aren't children anymore, Rian," I retort, my voice laced with bitterness. Because now I've seen the emptiness behind his facade. I won't let myself be tricked again.

Chapter

4

The cobblestone streets of the vampire district glisten under the lights, the air tinged with smoke and iron—a fitting backdrop for the nocturnal aristocracy that rule this land. Vampires have had domain over this part of the Aboveground—Oiche—since the fae war, when they sided with us over the Fomorians, the dark anti-fae. They had just enough savagery to keep them violent for our objectives, with immortality taken from our joint fae ancestors. I never considered why they chose us over our unrestrained fomorian cousins, but seeing Fuil now tells me the fae's demand for tradition, our cultivated society, may have had something to do with it.

Fuil is a place of opulent decay, and the very air thrums with an undercurrent of power. Vampires have no magic as we'd describe it, but they are beings of magic, able to live forever. Some of them, the born vampires known as the Aislean, have no limitations in the sun and can create other vampires, the Turned. Alas, the Turned live a half-life, always waiting for their time when the moon rises, and unable to create their own vampire fledglings, instead cursed to be secondary to the noble Aislean.

I feel for them.

With the sun just dipping into the earth, Rian and I weave through the aristocratic throng of the Aislean, our steps a synchronized dance born of necessity rather than intimacy. In any other circumstance, I'd love to be here. Perhaps, once the cuffs are off, I could—

"What do you think of Fuil?" Rian's melodic voice breaks into my thoughts.

I heave a begrudging sigh. "I have to admit, there's a certain allure to this district," I reply, aiming a sidelong glance at Rian.

The corners of Rian's lips curl into a devilish smirk as he leans in closer, his warm breath sending shivers down my spine. "Just like you, darling."

I elbow him hard in the gut, which I should have done when we were traveling from Heriot Island to the mainland. Better to nip these flirtations in the bud than let him keep riling me up for his own amusement.

"So violent," he hisses, rubbing his side. After a minute, he sidles close as the street is packed with passersby, and says, "You should accompany me on more of these visits. I must complete diplomatic visits in every sector here, more once I take the position of High King. You could explore to your heart's content while I do the tedious things. Unless, you'd prefer to complete those tedious chores for me," he teases.

I tuck a stray lock of hair behind my ear. The idea is tantalizing, intoxicating even, to imagine myself by his side, not just as a companion, but as a partner in all things political and personal. But such thoughts were emotionally treacherous; that role belonged to a queen, and I was far from wearing any crown.

"I think your Queen would probably prefer the former best friends remain back at Avalaruin," I finally say, offering a strained smile and putting more distance between us.

"Former," he starts, sounding affronted, but he's cut off as a vampire in too much of a hurry tries to slip into the space between us. He catches on our chain and nearly flips over.

The vampire snarls his irritation as we help him up and brush the dust from his frock. He marches away, his sharp complaints following behind him.

I wait until the street starts to clear and hold up my wrist just enough to let the manacle glint ominously in the lamplight. "Is there anything you can do to make these less conspicuous?" I ask. "Before we cause an international incident."

Rian's face contorts into a deep frown as he stares down at them. The flicker of the lamplight reflects off of them, not the warm gaslamps I'm used to but some human invention called elek-tricity, creating an eerie glow on his sharp features. "I'm afraid not, dearest," he says. "Glamour is a delicate art, but it cannot overcome pure magic."

I frown back at him. "Well, I'd rather not broadcast our predicament to every vampire we come across."

"I doubt they'll care," he says with a raised brow, as though my fears are unfounded.

"They could tell someone else," I explain, my voice growing heated. "You're the crown prince. Someone could recognize you and go tattling to the elders."

Which would, as I consider it further, be more embarrassing than anything else. No one would believe Rian willingly attached himself to me, much less consider me a threat to the crown. But it's another example of my oafishness; silly Sorcha and her silly magic. If I'm lucky, the elders wouldn't retaliate by trying to bind me to someone as bad as Jackson, and would instead take pity on the sad Sorcha and give me someone just as oafish.

"Come here," Rian murmurs, drawing me closer with a gentle tug. His hand slips deftly under the hem of my jacket, his fingers warm against the small of my back as he guides my hand beneath his coat. "Like this, if anyone asks, we're just two lovers out for a sunset stroll."

A blush creeps up my neck as one hand slips above the hem. But as he curls his fingers towards my hip, closer to my stomach, I freeze up. "Don't."

His hand quickly slides back to my back. "Alright, dearest. No harm meant." He glances down at our intertwined forms. "We do make quite the pair, don't we?" he remarks with a playful smile.

"Don't get used to it," I warn, the words sharper than I intended. My hands clench at my sides, unsure if the warning was meant for him or me.

We keep going, walking through Fuil until the sun finally sets. The streets are quiet now, the Aislean retreating to their homes as the darkness settles in, and it's too early for the Turned to yet awaken and come out to play in the moonlight.

"Although, loathe as I am to remove your hands from me, now that I finally have your touch again," Rian begins after another hour's march onward, his voice a velvet rumble that pulls at my senses despite my best efforts to remain unaffected. "I'm in dire need of reprieve. We've been up for hours, and even a crown prince needs his beauty sleep."

"Beauty sleep?" I snort softly. "But your ego appears as well-rested and robust ever."

He chuckles, his breath warm against my cheek. "Yes, such a need is mine alone. You're already gorgeous, even in the dead of night—or perhaps especially then. Would you let me see you in the dark and check for myself, dearest?"

I ignore his false attention, focusing instead on a nearby lamppost flickering with that otherworldly flame. "We can stop for the night, I suppose. Maybe find an open alley—"

His hand, the uncuffed one, flies to his chest. "An alley? I know this is your first time in Fuil, but surely you know there are inns here."

I shoot him a pointed look, exasperation simmering beneath the surface. "I know well that vampires have inns, Rian," I retort, my tone laced with irritation. "I'm not ignorant of basic vampire society."

Rian merely grins at my reaction, his eyes alight with mischief. "Of course not, my sharp-witted companion," he teases, the corners of his lips quirking up in a playful smile. "So shall we seek refuge in one of those fine establishments? Or would you truly prefer the charming ambiance of a dark alleyway?"

Before I can deliver a scathing reply, because *some* of us don't have the gold to spend at inns, Rian tugs me gently and leads the way down a side street lined with ornate iron lanterns that cast intricate shadows on the cobblestones below. The Black Rose Inn looms ahead, its façade a menacing blend of sharp spires and monstrous statues.

"This should do," Rian announces, holding open the door with a flourish. "After you, milady."

"Such chivalry," I murmur, passing by him with an anxious flutter in my chest. His charm is practiced, effortless, like the rest of him. It's a performance, but one I spent years being too eager to applaud. Now, it just leaves me bracing for the punchline.

We step into the inn where the lobby is an expanse of dark metal and crimson velvet, the air perfumed with a blend of incense and the faintest hint of blood wine. Tapestries in all colors fill the walls, with chandeliers above flickering from true flame, not the human's new version of it.

A tired-looking vampire behind the front desk greets us with a polite nod, his eyes flickering towards our closeness. "Good evening," he greets, his eyes reflecting the muted light. "One bed, I presume?"

"Actually—" I begin, mentally calculating how much of my savings I'll need to withdraw to pay for half a room, but Rian cuts me off.

"Yes, one bed will suffice," he says smoothly.

"Very well," the innkeeper replies, sliding a brass key across the counter. "Unfortunately, the bed is smaller than standard." He eyes us. "A bit cozy for the fae, that is. Your lot is usually bigger than us. I trust that won't be a problem?"

Rian accepts the key, his expression unreadable. "Not at all."

A tight knot forms in my stomach. There was a time when sharing Rian's bed was all I wanted, back when I still thought he could want me too. But now? It's a cruel test to my control and emotions, one I'm bound to fail.

Rian turns to me, the key glinting between his fingers. "Shall we?" he asks, his voice an irritating whisper of seduction and secrets.

His question lingers between us, casual but laden with undertones I refuse to acknowledge.

He's playing a game, but it's one I don't know the rules to anymore. My heart pounds, and I hate that it still reacts to him like this.

"After you," I answer, my heart a wild thing within its cage.

But he leads me up the narrow staircase to our shared room, his hand warm against my back. The door shuts behind us with a click that echoes too loudly in the close silence of the room. I swallow hard, my gaze lingering on the piece of furniture that seems to take up all the space in my head, but a slight thing inside the chamber, the bed draped in rich burgundy velvet and silk.

It's mocking me, this bed. The one thing I've sworn to avoid—binding, closeness, vulnerability—and here it is, wrapped in velvet and inevitability.

Turning from it, I light the lamps with a flick of my fingers. Rian makes an appreciative sound at my display of magic. I've always been good at lights, just not much else.

"I suppose we'll have to make do with what we have," he says, his voice low and husky.

"We could have gotten a better room," I tell him. "I could pay you back."

"Not to worry, darling. Just as with the clothes, because it is my magic that accepted your wish, I will fund this entire endeavor."

Why does he have to make even generosity sound like a flirtation?

I frown, opening my mouth to further argue, even though it *is* his fault, but no words come out as Rian slowly unbuttons his coat, revealing the sculpted lines of his clothed chest underneath. The sleeve catches at our wrists and without another thought, he rips it off, letting the torn fabric fall to the floor in a whisper. In the light of my magic, he looks even more ethereal, like a god come to life, the bright white of his tunic contrasting beautifully with his golden skin and wild black hair. I avert my gaze as I try to work off my jacket, but it catches on my shoulders.

Rian turns to face me fully, his fingers brushing against mine as he reaches for my jacket, the contact sending a jolt through me. I swallow hard, willing myself to maintain composure despite the chaos of desire swirling inside me.

"Let me help you with this," Rian murmurs, his voice a velvet caress that raises goosebumps on my skin. Heat radiates off his body, drawing me closer even as I want to step back. With soft hands, he slides my jacket off my shoulders.

"Don't tear it," I whisper, my voice breathier than I'd like. "It's the only one I have."

"I'll be gentle," he assures me, his fingers deftly working the fabric off my wrist and onto the chain.

In a whisper of movement, the jacket slips away to the floor. "An illusion," he explains, leaning in closer.

I'm about to question him on how the cuffs can be an illusion (and malleable) now but can't be magicked off, when he continues, "But if it isn't to your liking, I'll buy you an entirely new wardrobe."

"I wouldn't let you," I say, pursing my lips.

Rian watches me with a gentle intensity, his fingers lightly grazing my cheeks as if trying to memorize every freckle and curve. "I know, my beauty, you'll never accept something given to you. You must always take it for yourself." His voice is barely above a murmur as he lifts his gaze to meet mine. "Now, it is your turn," he whispers.

All thoughts of my own clothes vanish. Time seems to slow as the flickering light of my magic dances in his eyes. His words hang there, daring me to respond, to cross the invisible line I must keep drawn between us.

I should step away, regain the distance I've fought so hard to maintain. But instead, my gaze falls to his lips, parted ever so slightly, and I wonder how soft they might feel against mine. I fight the urge to reach out, to touch the forbidden silhouette of his jawline, to follow the curve of his lips. Instead, with trembling fingers, I trace the lines of his chest, feeling the steady rise and fall of his breath beneath my touch. There's a hunger in his eyes that mirrors my own, as I reach for the hem of his shirt. Grasping the hem, I pull the fabric up and over his head, revealing intricate black tattoos over his chest that seem to come alive in the flickering of my magic light.

As the fabric slips from his lean frame and he magicks it to the floor, he stands before me in all his glory, a sculpted work of art bathed in the soft glow of my light. His pants hang low, a thick bulge pressed tight against the fabric. My gaze wants to remain fixed there, but I drag it away, down his muscular thighs, the fabric straining there just as much as over his crotch.

He needs looser pants, I think almost hysterically. But I can't stop inspecting him, the golden skin of his chest, the intricate tattooed lines under his collarbones, the sharp angle of his shoulders, muscles that bunch as he shifts before me. At one point, seeing this, seeing him, was all I wanted. I try to steady myself, to push aside the overwhelming desire that threatens to unravel me with every passing second.

This is all just a distraction. I would experience this arousal with any attractive fae. As would he.

But I can't quite convince myself of that.

With a steady hand, Rian reaches out and traces a line from my clothed collarbone down to the curve of my waist, towards the hem of my shirt. Like a bucket of water thrown over my head, I take a step back, creating a safe distance between us. But Rian closes the gap almost immediately.

"You're beautiful," he murmurs, his voice filled with sincerity. "Even more so without all the layers." His fingers reach for my shirt again.

I clear my throat. "We should sleep," I say, my voice soft but resolute.

He inhales sharply, before offering a sharp smile. "Indeed," he finally agrees, his eyes searching mine with an intensity that feels like a touch. "It's been a long day for us both, I imagine."

Our pants come off with no ceremony or temptation, leaving us both in our scraps of underclothing. We retreat to the bed, both slipping beneath the cool sheets. The cuffs jangle between us, as I fall into a fitful sleep.

Chapter 5

Consciousness comes slowly, a faint glimmer of light behind my closed eyelids. I shift, an instinctive attempt to orient myself, and an unexpected warmth presses against my back. A body—a living, breathing presence emanating a heat that seeped into my chilled bones. I roll my shoulders, letting the comforting warm air cover the nape of my neck.

An arm wraps around me, pulling me closer towards the hard planes of a naked chest. The arm is muscled and tan, dusted with dark hair, with veins visible beneath the skin. A faint, pleasant scent wafts up from the exposed skin, a mix of fresh soap and a hint of pine.

Did I take someone home with me? I hadn't done that since after Jackson... No, not since Noel. Noel, who'd told me I was too closed off. Spitefully, I'd closed myself off more in the aftermath.

The man's breath tickles the curve of my ear, and he groans lightly. I inhale sharply, the intimate contact jolting memories back into focus. Tied. I was tied to someone. The arm around my waist is wrapped with a golden cuff, with a delicate chain snaking its way to circle around my hand resting beside me.

Rian.

My heart flutters, a bird suddenly aware of the cage surrounding it. *Did he draw me close or did my traitorous body search for his in the night?*

No matter the answer, I can't let it continue. I allow myself a single indulgence before planning to retreat: a deep breath filled with the scent of earth and woods that clings to Rian's skin. It's a heady aroma, mingling with the subtle musk of his natural essence. In another life, it might have been intoxicating, leading me down a path of yearning and desire. But this was not that life, and ours was not a bond forged by choice or passion. I'd taken this road before, and it led nowhere.

"Sorcha?" Rian's voice barely rises above a whisper. He stirs beside me, sending fresh waves of warmth coursing along my spine. His hand slips beneath the hem of my shirt and I stiffen, the idea of retreating forgotten when faced with the memories of what lies under that fabric.

"Not there. Please," I murmur, forcing a lightness into my tone to avoid any uncomfortable questions.

Rian groans softly. "Let me awaken and I promise I'll only touch where you desire." He shifts closer, twining his legs further around mine and pressing himself firmly against me.

And then there's something else pressing against me, just between the vee of my legs. Despite his comment about needing to awaken, some part of him is wide awake as the hard length of him nestles at the curve of my ass. I'd noticed it before, the thick length of it bulging from his pants, but to *feel* it.

Hells.

"Rian," I gasp, my voice laced with an urgency that could rouse the dead, turning to push him away. But his cock only seems to move closer.

I shouldn't be thinking about how nice that feels. How the idea of him flipping over and sliding between my legs sounds like a lovely way to wake up. I shift further.

Rian's eyelids flutter open, revealing eyes the color of a stormy sea. "I see this is the part of the morning where you touch *me* where I desire."

"Excuse me?" I snap, though the heat creeping up my neck betrays my feigned irritation. With how dry my throat is, I'm amazed I can even speak.

"You continue pushing back towards me, dearest," he says, leaning closer, his breath skimming over my cheek.

My gaze flicks towards our bodies without permission. Even that slight movement pushes my hips forward and my behind backward, rolling me further into him. His own body responds by inching even closer. The covers lift and I know he's looking down at our bodies, the way we're nearly molded together. With our pants off, there's only two small scraps of fabric preventing skin-on-skin contact there.

I can feel the pressure of him now, burning like a brand through the material, as if acknowledging it made it truly real. It's intoxicating, the way his body fits against mine.

"I've stopped. It's your turn now," I manage to say, asserting myself with a laugh that's only half-convincing. Embarrassment wants to burn through me but his proximity ignites a different heat—fire meeting tinder, threatening to consume all reason.

"To better touch you? I agree," he growls. He grinds more firmly into me, his hand squeezing my hip as he ruts against me, thrusting in rhythmic strokes.

A moan escapes me as I move with him, feeling him push against me, arousing me more than I thought possible. As if not in control of my limbs, one hand reaches behind me to touch the rim of his ear, the other clenching Rian's arm around my stomach. The tinkling of our intertwined chain reminds me of the reality between us.

"We need to free ourselves," I state firmly, though my voice trembles with want. Slowly, I untangle myself from his embrace.

"Let me free you," he says, his face against my hair, dragging his lips down to the back of my neck, refusing to let me leave the bed, banding me in his arms again. "Let me give you a release, darling."

The temptation hangs between us like a heavy fog, seductive and dangerous. This can't be happening, the man I loved for years cannot be here offering himself to me. Desire mingles with apprehension inside me.

Is this just another one of his games? Just like yesterday, just like always?

But don't I deserve it? Just once before whatever fate awaits me on Lughnasadh?

"Rian," I breathe out, his name both a plea and a warning.

He grinds against me again. "I'm here, darling. Whatever you wish, I'm always here, wanting you."

The snarled words are like a bucket of ice water poured over my skin.

I WAS SIXTEEN YEARS old.

The grand hall of Rian's castle glittered with enchantment as the fae gathered for the Lughnasadh celebration. Several couples were going to bind tonight. As a young fae, I thought the idea was romantic: binding to your love, or binding to one you could someday love. Time taught me otherwise.

That night, I stood at the edge of the ballroom, watching the chandeliers and the shimmering magic that danced in the air. The room was alive with laughter and music, but I couldn't connect with any of it. I had come here for one reason only: Rian.

Since Mama died the year before, I'd found solace in Rian's company. We spent hours talking, finding comfort in each other's presence. But things changed. Rian's mother had died just a few weeks ago, and though I wanted to be there for him, I hadn't seen him since.

Standing alone in my delicate blue gown, I searched the crowded ballroom for Rian among the sea of young fae. Finally, I caught sight of him near the center of the room, surrounded by a group of friends. He looked as handsome as ever, his dark hair tousled and falling down to his shoulders now. His piercing eyes seemed to hold all the secrets of the universe. To my sixteen-year-old self, they held all the secrets of my heart.

My chest tightened as I watched him laugh at something one of his friends said.

He seemed so effortlessly at ease, while I felt like I was drowning in a sea of emotions. Taking a deep breath to calm myself, I made my way towards him. But every time I got close, he slipped away like a shadow. It was as if he was purposely avoiding me, and it hurt more than I could admit.

Frowning in confusion and teenaged angst, I followed him as he retreated to the edge of the ballroom. Determined to speak to him, I pushed through the crowd until I was standing by his side. But as soon as I opened my mouth to speak, he glanced nervously around the room and moved away again.

Finally, I stopped. Untalented with magic didn't mean unintelligent. I wouldn't chase him further. I spent the rest of my evening by a large pillar, leaning against it and watching the scene before me. The other fae were dancing and laughing, lost in their own world of magic and merriment. It was something I wanted to experience, but I'd always been an introvert; since Mama's death, I became even more isolated.

"Sorcha."

I turned at the sound of my name, finding Rian standing a few feet away from me. His usually bright eyes were darker now, shadows of grief lingering in their depths.

"Hi, Rian," I said softly. All offense at his running from me was forgotten in his presence. "I—I'm sorry about your mother."

"Thanks," he replied with a small nod, his gaze flicking downwards. "I haven't meant to ignore you. I'm sorry I've been... distant."

My heart ached at the vulnerability in his voice. I stepped closer, reaching out to touch his arm. "It's okay, Rian. I understand."

He looked up at me then, his searching gaze meeting mine. "I just... miss her so much. And I don't know how to deal with it."

I nodded, my own eyes wanting to fill with tears. "I know. I miss Mama, too. It's hard."

Rian took a deep breath, his hand reaching up to cup my cheek. "You're always so strong, Sorcha. As if you can handle anything. I don't..." He appeared to steel himself. "I've no idea what I'd do without you."

But still... a part of me wanted to rail about his fickleness. He'd been avoiding me all night, literally running away at times. But the overwhelming part of my teenage heart wanted to relish what I had of him. He was my everything, the object of my immutable childish heart. I leaned into his hand, my eyes closing briefly. "I'm always here for you, Rian. Always." *I would choose you, I would have you*, I meant.

He took a step closer, our bodies almost touching. My breath hitched as I stared up at him. He'd gotten so tall. I knew he'd end up towering over me by the time of his majority. I wished he would kiss me, to take me in his arms, and let me hold him.

"Sorcha," Rian whispered, his voice thick with emotion.

Before I could respond, he leaned down and pressed his lips to mine. The world seemed to fall away, a rush of warmth and magic coursing through me. My hands grasped the front of his shirt, pulling him closer. It was everything I had ever dreamed of, the kiss soft and tender, filled with all the unspoken words between them. The world fell away: no party, no fae, no sadness. Just us, Rian and Sorcha. At last.

His hands slid around my waist, pulling me even closer as he deepened the kiss. I poured all my love and longing into the kiss, hoping he could feel it, hoping he understood.

But all too soon, Rian pulled away, his breath ragged. He rested his forehead against mine, his eyes closed. "Sorcha, that was…"

"Rian, I—" I began, but I was cut off by a voice calling out over the music.

"Rian! There you are!"

We turned, still wrapped up in each other's arms, to see Isabel hurrying towards them, her expression one of concern. Rian's eyes flickered with something I couldn't quite place.

"I have to go," Rian said, his voice strained. "Isabel needs me." He stepped away, his hands slipping from my waist.

"Oh… okay." I offer him a wincing smile. "I hope everything is alright."

"I'm sorry," he replied. "I'll talk to you later, I promise."

And he turned and walked away with Isabel, leaving me standing there, my heart wanting to shatter. I watched them go, and I waited another hour for him to find me 'later,' like he'd promised.

He never did.

By the time the party ended, a sense of emptiness settled over me. I had wished for a kiss, and Rian had granted it. But as I stood alone in the grand hall, I couldn't shake the feeling that it had all been a mistake. That Rian had only kissed me out of pity, *because* of the wish, to give me what I wanted in a moment of vulnerability. The realization cut deep, and I buried my feelings a little deeper that day.

"WHERE DID YOU GO?" Rian rumbles, pressing closer to me and kissing down my neck as I shut my eyes tight against the memories.

To a time where I learned what disappointment was.

"Sorcha, darling." His hips continue to move in a steady rhythm as a moan escapes from his own mouth. "Please."

Do I allow myself this? The knowledge of it and his touch?

Will it only hurt worse?

My gaze falls upon the clothes we had discarded on the floor last night, his torn coat and my pristine jacket.

"I want you to touch me," I whisper through heavy breaths.

"Anywhere, love, I will," he promises, his voice low and smooth, like honey poured over a wound. "Just tell me where. Say it aloud. Not a wish. Let there be no mistake."

"I want you to touch my cunt," I tell him. "And give me release right now."

"Hells, Sorcha," he sighs, kissing my clothed shoulder. "At your command."

His chained wrist drags over my torso, roaming over my breasts before riding down the curves of my stomach. I arch my back and let my hand reach around to pull his hair, forcing his lips towards the skin revealed from the neck of my shirt. He obliges, giving the soft contour of my neck a kiss, skimming his tongue over the skin, slow and wet. And then finally, his hand slides low beneath the covers and slips between my legs.

My body quakes with an involuntary shudder. It hasn't been that long, but knowing it's Rian's hand, his lips against my neck, fills me with wildfire. Those sinuous fingers curl against my core, slipping into my cunt. It almost hurts with how good it feels and I push back and forth again, letting the heel of his hand rub against me while his fingers dip in and out of my wet heat. He gasps as I increase my rubbing, chasing the high of his hands, letting his fingers sink in and out. And I remember the hard length of him only a scrap of fabric away.

Quickly, I release his hair. He makes a soft noise that turns into a deep groan as I frantically twist to shove my hand between us, slipping beneath the fabric hugging his waistline.

"Fuck," he moans as I maneuver to wrap my palm around his thick cock. "This is my wish instead, is it?"

I laugh, but it's cut off by a whine as something burns in my core, rising through my stomach like high tide. In a daze, I stroke his throbbing length in time with his questing fingers. It's cramped, stunted, but the noises he makes tell me he doesn't care.

"Oh, love—this is—" he says, the words sounding slurred as he groans them into my neck. "Want this, did you? Gods know it."

He presses open mouth kisses over all the skin he can reach, his other hand, pinned between us, grabbing my thick thigh. His fingers push in and out again, sparking lightning as he does it over and over until I'm sweating, forearm burning as I keep pace with him.

Until my back arches, and everything flashes white, body rigid. The low lights I lit the night before flash until they explode into an eruption of sparks. He groans as I shatter, thrusting raggedly into my hand as I come.

And then it's quiet. And dark, only the fragmented light from the curtains illuminating us. There's something wet behind me, he must have come too. He slips his fingers from my cunt; they glisten in the morning light. I lift a corner of the covers for him to wash off, but he sticks his fingers in his mouth instead. I turn to watch his expression, his eyes fluttering closed as he licks the taste of me off his hand.

"Excellent plan, darling," he says, his eyes still shut tight. His body slumps back into the bed. "Avoid wishing and simply demand it from me, darling, and we'll never be in a predicament like the cuffs again."

At the reminder, at the confirmation this is all a transaction still, I let the door close between us again.

Chapter 6

Our journey to the Oracle's lair begins with a trek through the dark and foreboding woods just to the south of Fuil. We must make our way through the forest until we reach Solindria Mountains, where the Oracle can be found. We'd dressed quickly, at my demand, and left the Inn.

Something about that exchange made me feel... unseemly. It wasn't a wish exactly, and he'd wanted it, he'd asked me for it but... it left me cold, annoyed. Rian had attempted to kiss me as we'd dressed, but I'd pushed him aside. He'd been aroused because he was in bed with a curvy female. He'd have done the same for any of the fae back home. Even the sirens, I bet. He wasn't here because he wanted to be, I'd need to remember that.

The forest air we walk through is thick with an ominous stillness, interrupted only by the crunch of leaves and twigs beneath our boots. As we make our way deeper into the forest, the towering trees seem to close in around us, their gnarled bark reaching out like grasping fingers. Despite Rian's assurances that there are no errant vampires in these woods, I can't shake off the feeling of being watched. Every rustle in the underbrush sets my heart racing, and I grip the hilt of my dagger tighter, ready for any potential danger.

"Rian," I say, breaking the tense silence that shrouds us like a thick cloak. "Couldn't you use your wish magic to get us there instantly?"

He hesitates before answering, his voice laced with something I can't quite decipher. "My powers have limitations, Sorcha. It's not as simple as granting a wish."

I glance at him. Certainly, he's failed to answer wishes before, but because of his own whims, nothing external. He's the crown prince, for pity's sake. He and the nobles are nearly godlike with their magical skill. He answers the wishes he wants, the one he asks for, like the orgasm this morning. And damn the rest of them. "*You* have limitations?"

"I can't undo this wish, for one," he reminds me, his gaze fixed on the path ahead. "But wishes are almost like contracts. You wish for us to go to the Oracle, and I grant it, what if that means we can go nowhere else? That I take us there and there we remain for eternity." A wry smile touches his lips, but his eyes remain cold, bothered. "And that is a rather unfettered, broad wish. I've heard wishes begging me for something a single time, just this once, Rian, they'd claim; answering it could mean I'd never see them again, because they got all they wanted from me."

I nod, though I don't fully understand. He granted my so-called binding wish without worrying about the temporal aspect.

I blanch. *Unless that was a hint and once we're unbound, we'll never see each other again.* What were my words again? I'd give anything to bind to Rian. Did I inadvertently overcomplicate my future?

I suppose it might make the fallout at the end of it easier. At least I got an orgasm out of it.

We walk in silence again, the only sounds the whispering of the trees and the occasional call of a distant bird. I focus on the crunching beneath my feet, letting the repetitive noise ground me.

A sudden rustling in the underbrush jolts me from my quiet contemplation. Rian leaps in front of me, his hand reaching for the hilt of his sword. Tension crackles in the air as we wait with bated breath, anticipating the source of the disturbance.

"Keep your wits about you, Sorcha," he cautions, the usual banter in his tone replaced by a steely edge.

Swallowing hard, my throat tightens at the thought of what could be lurking in the underbrush, the taste of fear appearing on my tongue. My magic certainly can't protect us. I clutch the hilt of the dagger at my belt—a slight comfort against the unknown threats of the forest. Rian's presence is a steady force beside me, but even he can't stop the anxiety that flutters in my chest with every rustle of leaves. We move with cautious steps, a silent agreement passing between us to be prepared for any danger that might lurk behind the next tree or beneath the next leaf.

Then, without warning, a guttural snarl cuts through the silence, and we spin toward the sound. Out of the corner of my eye, I glimpse movement—a flash of fur and glinting eyes. Before I can further react, a massive wolf emerges, its fur bristling and amber eyes fixed on us.

"Behind me, Sorcha!" Rian commands, stepping forward with a protective ferocity. His hand flares with an azure light, the manifestation of his wish magic ready to be wielded against our foes.

I obey immediately, my heart pounding in my chest as I watch the wolf circle us, its muscles tensed and ready to strike.

"Can you make us invisible?" I hiss.

Rian stands firm, his stance one of practiced determination, a lone warrior against the wild. "It would still smell us. If Isobel were here—"

The growl that comes next could be from either me or the wolf. But it homes Rian's focus back. The wolf circles cautiously, its gaze darting between us. But Rian's confidence is like a shield, deflecting the creature's aggression even as it lunges forward with bared teeth. I flick my wrist and bring about my lights, hoping a brief blinding will take the wolf from our trail.

"Wish for something, Sorcha. And make it precise," Rian demands, his lips barely moving. I step forward and begin my internal prayers. *Keep us unharmed, get the wolf away from us.*

The wolf stops, likely weighing the odds of a successful attack. But its hesitation was momentary, and with a snarl, it launches itself at Rian—a blur of fangs and claws seeking to tear through flesh. But Rian is quicker, sidestepping the assault with fluid grace. The air crackles with electric energy as Rian channels his power, a dazzling display of magic that dances between his fingertips. His magic surges forth in a brilliant arc of light, striking the wolf squarely in the chest.

The world appears to spin, a dizzying blur of shadow and snarls. The wolf tries again, leaping towards me. Rian's magic clashes with it, but I can't get out of the way in time, the force of that azure blue fire colliding from my stomach. Air whooshes from my lungs, the sound wrenched from my throat in a silent gasp. I double over, pain splintering through me like lightning, my silly little lights bursting open like overheated glass. The wolf tumbles backward with a yelp, running away.

"Sorcha!" Rian's voice is laced with terror. Magic still crackles around him, but his focus is narrowed to the space where I stand. "I should have granted that first wish, but I feared for the repercussions as it wasn't precise enough. Damnit!"

"It's fine," I tell him, pressing against the space below my breasts, where the heat of his magic struck. "I'll likely have a bruise from the fall. That's all."

"Let me see," he urges, desperation threading his tone as he kneels beside me. His hands hover over my stomach, hesitant but filled with the need to help.

I shake my head, a futile gesture to stop him. "No, it's nothing. Just—"

But he won't be swayed. His fingers slip beneath my shirt. I tense, not out of embarrassment, but from the instinct to shield myself from exposure.

"Sorcha, my love," Rian murmurs. He finds no bruises from the hit, only spots that will reveal themselves until later. But he discovers the silvered lines that mapped my hips, those that appeared as I developed too fast. "These are beautiful, proof of your curves."

A laugh, half-irritation, half-disbelief, bubbles up, as I try to yank my shirt back down. "I'm not ashamed," I insist, my voice steady even as my body trembled from the aftershocks of the blow. "You should see the lines on my breasts."

I've always been 'more to love,' but I considered myself a bastion of supple femininity that any man should be thrilled to touch. Except... I didn't always feel that way—young Sorcha had to learn and even current Sorcha needs reminding—but those stretch marks weren't what I was hiding beneath my shirt.

"I would, darling," Rian says with an insincere leer, fighting against me covering myself and trying to trace a path along the ridges of my skin. "But so far you've kept that luscious part of your body hidden from me."

His hands still, and he's found what I was concealing, the long jagged line that further mars my skin. The fabric flies upward, revealing the cruel souvenir from a past not easily forgotten. His fingers hover over the raised scar, tracing the outline without touching, as if even the air between might be too harsh for old wounds.

"Who did this to you?" he asks, his voice no louder than the rustle of leaves underfoot.

I shift uncomfortably. "Jackson's handiwork," I finally admit, the words tasting bitter on my tongue. Jackson was cruel, I'd said. He didn't only leave me with emotional scars.

I watch as Rian's jaw tightens, the muscles of his neck taut with restrained fury. The surrounding air seems to hum with his barely leashed power—wish magic that simmered beneath the surface, seeking an outlet for his wrath.

"Rian, please," I say, reaching out to lay a hand upon his clenched fist. "It's in the past. It doesn't matter."

But my reassurance is a spark to kindling. "It matters to me," he growls, his protective instincts a tangible force. "This... This is why you fear being bound?"

I nod, the reality of my vulnerability laid bare between us. "You're exposed to that person, to their demands, and I've had enough of weakness."

His gaze softens, his anger giving way to something akin to understanding. "Sorcha," he whispers, his voice softening. "Your strength lies in your scars, in the battles you've fought and survived. And I swear to you, I will never cause such wounds on your skin or your heart."

The image of him, as my protector, promising me safety, cracks like the glass table Jackson had shoved me into. Rian has already scarred my heart.

"I'm sure," I reply, offering a wincing smile, trying to hide my doubt. "We should keep going," I urge, more to convince myself than him. "We have an Oracle to seek and answers to find."

With a nod, Rian steps back, allowing me space yet remaining close enough that the warmth of his body chases away the chill that crept through the woods. It can't, of course, remove the chill the memory of my past bindings inspired.

THE REST OF THE walk to the Oracle's den is uneventful, though my mind churns with unease. There was no morning release when we awoke this morning, and not only because we needed to spend shifts sleeping to avoid being surprised by another wolf. Luckily we move so much faster than the humans do, or I'd have been stuck on this trek for weeks.

We come upon our prize as the sun crests above us, the cavern's mouth appearing as a gateway framed by entwined roots and moss-draped stones. Stepping over the threshold, it feels as though we crossed into another realm entirely, the air vibrating with a palpable, thrumming energy that quickens my pulse and sends shivers cascading down my spine.

"Keep your wits about you," I whisper, echoing Rian's earlier words as much as my own need for it.

Inside, the Oracle's dwelling unfurls like a waking dream. Crystals jut from crevices, gleaming as though very stars had been plucked from the sky and embedded into the earth. A myriad of candles flicker, their flames undulating gently. The magic here is as real as the beat of our hearts, an ancient song that hums through the veins of the Aboveground, a reminder that some wonders refuse to stay hidden in the land of the fae.

I can scarcely breathe, the enchantment so thick around us that it seems to press against my skin. "How can such magic exist here, Aboveground?" I murmur, more to myself than to Rian, who remains a silent sentinel beside me.

"Because, child," a voice echoes, "true magic knows no bounds, not of land nor sky."

From the shadows, the Oracle emerges, her form as fluid as mist rising from the forest floor at dawn. She's draped in fabrics that shimmer with their own inner light, her eyes pools of knowledge that seem to pierce through the veil of my soul. There, I swear I see a glimpse of eternity, a connection to something greater than myself, a conduit for the secrets of the universe.

Which I pray means she is a conduit for the secret to unbinding me from Rian.

"Oracle," I begin. "We've journeyed far to seek your wisdom. We are bound, Rian and I, by chains neither of us wished for." He makes an injured noise, but I silence him with a sharp gesture, tinkling the chain. I hold it up to the Oracle's sight. "Tell us, please, how do we break these bonds?"

Her gaze holds mine, ageless and inscrutable. "Seek you freedom, or understanding, Sorcha of Avalaruin?" she asks, her words threading through the silence with the precision of an arrow.

"Freedom," I breathe. I know how the bond was forged. I don't need understanding, only release.

"Then know this," the Oracle says, her hands weaving patterns in the air, trailing luminescence like stardust in her wake. "Only completion will unbind you. That which has been set in motion must come full circle. Only then will the chains fall away."

The flickering candlelight dances across Rian's features, casting shadows along the sharp angles of his jaw, the intensity in his eyes unwavering. "Completion," he echoes, the word hanging between us like an unspoken promise.

I swallow back the frustration that knots within me. "But what must we complete?" The answer seems so close and yet slips through my grasp, as elusive as the dark shapes playing across the cave walls.

The Oracle's eyes gleam with the light of a thousand stars, her ethereal form seeming to blur at the edges as if she were more apparition than a being of flesh and blood. "The threads of life are tangled around you, Sorcha of Avalaruin," she whispers, her voice carrying the weight of centuries. "To unbind yourselves, you must walk the path that truth has carved for you. Find that which lies at the heart of your bond, and there you shall find your completion."

I frown. The chain between us is even heavier against my skin with the non-answer pulling it down. Beside me, Rian remains silent, his features drawn tight in concentration as he absorbs the Oracle's words.

The Oracle glides closer to him, drawing his gaze towards her towering form. "And you, Rian not-yet-High King. Ask yourself this: when the games end, will you be the winner or the loser?"

He shakes his head, like he's shaking off a dream. "My victory is assured," he replies, his voice resolute, though I catch a flicker of doubt in his eyes.

The Oracle's gaze pierces through him, likely seeing beyond the facade of confidence he wears like armor. "Winning isn't always about what you gain, but what you're willing to lose," she says cryptically.

Rian's jaw tightens as the Oracle fades from our view.

We step out of the Oracle's dwelling and a heavy silence settles between us. Rian appears focused on his own cryptic message, but everything he does is a game, so I set my curiosity at what was revealed aside. Instead, I turn over the words from the Oracle, teasing them through my mind. *Completion and heart of the bond.* Further binding myself is terrifying, willfully choosing to toss aside every scrap of freedom I've clung to.

We walk for hours before Rian finally breaks the silence between us, his voice pitched low but resolute. "Completion," he begins, his gaze intense as it meets mine. "I think I know what she means by that." Anticipation tingles down my spine at the raw edge of his words.

"Tell me," I prompt, my heart thundering in my chest like a captive bird seeking freedom. Whatever it is, I'll do it. Anything to get away from the emotional maelstrom that comes from being this close to Rian again.

He takes a step closer, the subtle scent of pine and earth emanating from him like a primal allure. "I believe... completion means more than just unraveling the heart of our bond, but a... coming together," he muses, his voice laced with seductive intent.

My pulse races at his insinuation, and I find myself caught in the depths of his eyes. The air crackles with an unspoken tension, a silent understanding passing between us like an invisible current.

"Are you suggesting..." I start, my voice no more than a whisper, "that completion could mean..."

His fingers trace a line down my jaw, sending shivers cascading down my spine. "That perhaps we should retreat to another inn, darling."

Chapter 7

THE WORDS HOVER IN the air between us, a precarious promise or... yet another game he loves playing.

"You're impossible," I mutter, though my voice falters. "We'll keep thinking. There must be something else." Completion could mean so many things.

Before he can reply, the forest shifts from the dusky calm to a sudden storm of movement and steel. Vampires, clad in the dark livery of the royal guard, materialize from the encroaching shadows, their swords unsheathed and gleaming with lethal purpose.

Rian steps forward, his body shielding mine as the point of a sword inches closer to us. He flashes a roguish grin, disarmingly nonchalant amidst the looming threat. His stance is loose, almost careless, but there's an undercurrent of readiness, a coiled spring waiting for reason to release. One hand rests against the hilt of his sword, the other sparks blue.

"Easy, friends," he says, his voice a silken thread woven through the palpable unease. "You ought to save your steel for the wolves prowling your borders. We fae are far less bite and all bark."

The guards hesitate, their expressions veiled behind the masks of duty, yet I sense their confusion, the subtle shift of weight from heel to toe.

"Rian," I hiss, my voice laced with both annoyance and anxiety. "Be serious for once."

"This is me serious," he says with a wink.

A silence falls, thick and heavy as velvet drapery, as someone steps out from the shadows. A male vampire that moves with lethal grace, his beauty a sharp-edged weapon that seems to carve the shadows away with each step. Reflected light caresses his alabaster skin, glinting off the ruby brooch at his throat—the sigil of the queen, if I remember my studies. His eyes, two pools of liquid onyx, find mine. But Rian doesn't let the attention linger.

"Phaeron, lovely to see you," Rian says, stepping forward with a confidence that borders on recklessness. "Who knew our little stroll through the mountains would lead to such grand company?"

The vampires surrounding us remain stoic, their swords held at the ready, unmoved by Rian's attempts at humor. The stunning male vampire—Phaeron—regards Rian with an odd mixture of disdain and delight before turning his attention back to me, cocking his head and letting his pale blond hair cascade down to his shoulder. His gaze is intense, searching, as if trying to unravel the enigma of my existence with a mere look. I resist the urge to squirm under his scrutiny.

"The Queen demands your presence," Phaeron says, voice smooth as aged wine. His gaze shifts to Rian, and the corner of his mouth quirks upward in a semblance of a smile. "Immediately."

Rian chuckles. "Tell Her Majesty we're flattered by her urgency. I must admit, these woods do carry their own risks. But more so for her Aislean vampires than the fae." He picks up a fallen twig and examines it theatrically. "One can never be too cautious; sticks have a habit of turning into stakes if you're not paying attention."

"Rian!" I hiss, my heart hammering against my ribcage. If we're murdered by the royal guards in Fuil, there'll be no more worrying about the damn cuffs, at least.

Phaeron's lips twitch, a shadow of amusement flickering across his features before vanishing. Perhaps even the undead aren't immune to Rian's particular brand of charm.

"Your humor is noted," Phaeron replies dryly. "But I assure you, the only danger you currently face is the displeasure of our queen."

"But her displeasure can take *many* forms," Rian retorts, tossing the twig aside. It twirls through the air, landing with a soft thud among the leaves. The guards flinch, the swords jutting closer. "And I find the prospect of facing Demara far more daunting than any pointed stick."

I reach out, my fingers brushing against Rian's wrist in a silent plea for seriousness, the cuffs clinking together.

"Stop it," I murmur, though my words were meant for both men. "We will follow."

Rian grins, all charm and audacity as he makes a sweeping gesture with one hand. "Of course, love. Lead the way, Phaeron. I'm helpless to refuse a beautiful lady's request."

I shoot him a warning glare, but he merely winks back at me.

Phaeron nods once, sharply, and turns on his heel, leading us deeper into the forest towards a cavalcade of horses. In the distance, the castle of Fuil looms—a tiny silhouette of spires and gargoyles etched against the sky. I'd always wanted to visit, but it remains to be seen whether I'll enjoy it under these terms.

I AM *NOT* ENJOYING it.

The damp stone of the dungeon wall presses cold against my back as I slide down to sit on the hard floor, my gaze fixed on the harsh lamplight across the corridor. The minute we crossed the stone threshold of the castle, Phaeron directed the guards to toss us in the dungeons. That was likely hours ago now, but the dungeons provide no windows for me to check. The cold seeping through the stone is my only hint that night has fallen. I draw my knees to my chest, wrapping my arms around them in a futile attempt to conserve what little heat my body clings to.

Throughout our capture, Rian keeps up a steady stream of banter that seemed to bounce off the walls like restless spirits. "You know," he says casually, his voice echoing in the icy stillness, "I've always found dungeons to be terribly unfashionable. Not a single window to let in the moonlight!"

My glare is withering, but he flashes me a rakish grin, as if daring me to find humor in our predicament. The predicament he put me in.

"All I wanted, all I was attempting, was to get myself off the betrothal lists," I mutter into my knees. A yank brings Rian's chained wrist closer so I can better curl into myself. "To protect myself. To live alone without a monster of a husband chosen for me so I wouldn't have to abscond to the Aboveground."

"Well, now you can check Fuil off your list of destinations," Rian says, sounding as though he's offering reasonable advice. "You've seen the woods, the city, the dungeons."

"This isn't a sightseeing trip, Rian," I whisper. "This isn't how I'd choose it."

"Cheer up, love. These dungeons aren't so bad once you get used to the ambiance."

"Get used to it?" My words, when they come, are a hiss of barely contained fury. "Rian, I can't believe you. This is... this is all your fault. All of it."

His eyes flicker to mine, glinting like stars in the dim light. "My fault? Do recall you were the wisher here." He points to himself. "I am but a humble wish granter."

"I didn't wish! I had a half-hearted thought that you cobbled together some half-heard wish, you cuffed us together without a way to remove it, forcing our hand into coming to the Aboveground." I spit out the words, each one laden with accusation. "And... and you were rude to the guards!"

"I rather think the vampire guards found my wit quite charming," he says with infuriating nonchalance.

"Charming?" I echo incredulously, the sting of tears born of frustration threatening to breach my eyes.

"As always," he replies, his gaze focused on the iron-banded door.

I open my mouth to retort, to chastise him for his flippancy, but the grinding shriek of hinges cuts me off. The door swings open with purpose, and there, framed by metal torchlight, stands the vampire who must be Queen Demara. I've only seen portraits, the last from ten years ago before I stopped using Rian's library, but she looks the same, her beauty both ethereal and deadly. Silken locks of midnight hair cascade over her shoulders, and her eyes, like twin sapphires, blaze with authority. In the right light, she could be Rian's pale twin.

"Rian!" she exclaims, her voice a melody laced with venom. "You dare arrive unannounced? You know I dislike surprises."

"Ah, Demara, my queen, surely you know by now—I live to displease you," Rian quips, rising to meet her gaze, a cocksure smirk blooming.

I watch in horror as his brazenness draws a low chuckle from her.

She saunters closer, the subtle swish of her emerald gown a hypnotic rhythm. "Such insolence," she murmurs, leaning in close enough that her breath ghosts over his cheek. "It's a wonder no one has snuffed it out yet."

"Demara, don't pretend you don't enjoy it," Rian replies with a leer.

"And what, pray tell, is this unexpected visit for? Or should I guess it's something to do with these charming handcuffs?"

Her slender finger traces the cold metal that binds us, her touch igniting sparks along my skin.

Rian chuckles. "Let's just say they're part of the surprise."

"Surprise or not," Demara purrs. "One might mistake your intentions as... binding."

"Only if one has a penchant for leaping to salacious conclusions," he shoots back, his eyes dancing with delight.

I blink, missing half the innuendo and unable to discern whether Rian is making it better or worse. He's certainly living up to my image of him as a man who will flirt with anything, with or without a pulse.

"Salacious? Rian, you wound me. I am the epitome of propriety," Demara teases, her lips curling into a wry smile. "It is my sister who might let you play such."

I shift uncomfortably, the stones beneath me unforgiving. "Your...Majesty," I say, unable to contain my unease. "Why are we here?"

"Patience, little fae," she replies, turning her piercing gaze upon me. "All will be revealed in due time. For now, enjoy the hospitality of my dungeons."

"Such graciousness," Rian murmurs. "Remind me to return the favor at our next encounter."

The air between them crackles with a tension that was both menacing and intimate—a storm of wills that threatens to consume us all.

"Be careful, Rian," Demara warns with a playful glint in her eye. "Return the favor, and you may enjoy my accommodations far longer than you'd like. A few hundred years here may bore the cheek from you."

"Enough," I say, my voice steady despite the tremor threatening to reveal my nerves.

"Sorcha," Rian says, his voice low and steady. "It's fine. Trust me."

But I ignore him, stepping forward and placing myself between Rian and the tempest of the queen's wrath. "Your Majesty, we have no wish to offend. I wasn't aware we needed to present ourselves to you when we crossed the border. We simply needed to see the Oracle."

Demara's gaze turns calculating as she regards me. "The Oracle? Were you not aware such visits required accommodation from me?" She turns back to Rian. "The crown prince would know that. Guards!"

The dungeon door creaks open again, this time revealing a pair of imposing guards clad in dark armor. Their eyes bear into us with an intensity that sends a shiver down my spine. Rian, to my surprise, remains unfazed, his posture relaxed and his expression almost playful.

"Wait, please," I beg as the guards approach us. A surge of panic rises within me, knowing that I had unwittingly stepped into a power play between Rian and the enigmatic vampire queen. My heart thuds, the backdrop to the crisis unfolding.

Thump. The guards' hands clamp onto Rian's shoulders with unnerving precision.

Thump. They pull him to his feet, their grip unyielding.

Thump. I stumble after him, the chain binding us leaving me no choice.

Thump. One of the guards reaches for his sword, the metallic rasp of the blade being drawn sending a chill down my spine.

Thump. Rian tilts his head, baring his neck, a faint smirk playing on his lips as if daring them to strike.

Thump—Demara's laughter pierces the oppressive silence, sharp and melodic. It echoes off the stone walls, shattering the tension like fragile glass.

The guards immediately release Rian, stepping back as if retreating from some unspoken command. Rian, ever the performer, throws his head back and joins her in her laughter, his mirth as audacious as it is unsettling.

"What—what just happened?" The words spill out of me in a whisper, my chest heaving as though I'd forgotten to breathe.

Rian turns to me, his eyes alight with mischief. "Sorcha, you should have seen your face," he says, his grin infuriatingly broad.

I can only stare, my pulse pounding in my ears, torn between relief and the urge to throttle him.

"Priceless," Demara exclaims, her laughter like tinkling bells in the cold, dark dungeon. "Oh, Rian, you never fail to entertain."

Rian grins as he gives a mock bow. "Anything for your amusement, my queen. Although you almost had me believing it. I thought Raken was actually going to slice me open."

"I've been taking classes in the theatrical arts," a guard says gruffly. Rian claps him on the shoulder.

"It shows, good man, it—"

"What's going on?" I snap.

"Dear Sorcha, you truly are a delight," Demara says, her voice honeyed yet laced with steel. "Although, it seems my jest has unsettled you. Fear not, there will be no reprisal for your visit. Thank you, Raken and Jeralt. Please wait in the hall while we finish up."

I watch in bewilderment as the guards retreat, their departure leaving behind an uneasy silence that is quickly filled by Rian's insufferable chuckling. He steps closer to me, his hand resting lightly on my shoulder in a gesture that is both comforting and infuriating.

"Demara and I," Rian begins, "we have this little game. Last time I was here, on official fae business, I *might* have replaced her royal goblets with ones that—let's just say—weren't quite fit for a queen."

"I thought I needed a nursemaid," Demara adds.

"Her reaction was hilarious. So, naturally, she couldn't let that go unanswered. Hence, our grand reception and subsequent stay in these luxurious quarters." His grin is infectious, but I resist the urge to share in his amusement.

"This isn't my idea of fun, Rian." The cold air wraps around me like a cloak as I hug myself, trying to ward off the discomfort. My voice echoes faintly off the walls, a testament to the solitude our 'accommodations' offered.

"Sorcha, come now. You were not in any real danger." He reaches out, his hand brushing mine, sending warmth spiraling through me. Because of the cold and not his touch, that is. "I wouldn't have brought you here if I thought otherwise," he says, sounding earnest.

I pull away back towards the wall, the stone beneath my fingertips leeching away the fleeting warmth. "Your antics may amuse the undead, but I prefer my escapades without the threat of becoming part of the castle's architecture." I glance at the heavy iron door, half expecting it to creak open and reveal another twist in their irritating game.

Demara wipes a mirthful tear from her eye, composing herself with regal grace. "It seems your penchant for trouble has not waned, Rian."

Rian, his usual cavalier demeanor in full force, bows dramatically. "My dear queen, what can I say? Life is dreadfully dull without a bit of chaos."

"Don't punish Rian too harshly," Demara says to me, her voice softening. "The guards failed to tell me he had a beautiful guest with him, or else I would have released you sooner." She reaches forward and clasps her icy hands around my free one. "Let me make it up to you. Tonight, the castle is hosting the Blood Moon Ball. A night where the elite come to play, and I, your ever-gracious queen, will entertain potential suitors."

I gaze at Demara, her eyes shimmering with a mixture of mischief and sincerity. Rian stands beside me, his expression unreadable as he watches the exchange between the queen and me.

"Your Majesty, I... I'm not sure if I belong in such esteemed company. If I could, instead, visit your records room," I stammer, hiding the truth of it: that I'm not sure how long I want to remain in Fuil if this is how they treat 'guests.' And if I have the chance to review more records about the Oracle, it could only help understand what 'completion' truly means.

Demara's smile widens as she squeezes my hand gently. "Nonsense, my dear. You are a guest in my castle, a true guest now, and I would be honored to have you join us tonight. Consider it a gesture of goodwill amidst our little game with Rian."

"See, Sorcha? A night where fangs and finery come together in a spectacular display of elegance and bloodlust awaits. The perfect prelude to a completion," Rian says with a theatrical flourish.

When he drags his gaze back over me, there's a heavy expectation there, a reminder of the conversation from the forest that remains unfinished.

I glare at him as Demara watches us with a small smile.

"You are welcome to our records, of course," she says. "And perhaps I could tempt you with a new escort for this evening. There are many suitors for me but only one will take the crown. Any of the others would be lucky to have you on their arm."

"I highly doubt—" I begin but Demara cuts me off.

"If not royalty, I know you caught Phaeron's eye. As soon as I returned to the castle, he was abuzz about the gorgeous goddess attached to Rian."

My cheeks heat even as Rian's grip tightens on my shoulder.

"Sorcha has her escort tonight," he says sharply.

Demara's gaze flits between us, a knowing smile playing on her lips as if she holds secrets only she can unravel. "For tonight, certainly. But the night is not as long as we might want. And what say you, Rian? Care to join the ranks of the love-struck fools vying for my hand?"

My breath catches in my throat as I remember what I thought only days ago, how anyone would be lucky to bind to him. The Vampire Queen herself, if the elders would let him. As I consider the possibility of an inter-species alliance, the sharpness in Rian's gaze softens.

"While the thought of competing for your affection is undoubtedly tempting," he says, the corners of his mouth twitching. "I fear I must decline. I am simply waiting for my future queen to accept me." His hand squeezes my shoulder again.

I felt my breath catch, my pulse thrumming in my ears. Does he—

"Your loyalty is both touching and inconvenient," Demara says. "But perhaps it's for the best. I'd forgotten what we last discussed. Isabel was nearly giddy at the thought."

Isabel. The name is a cold splash of reality against the feverish heat of my thoughts. *Keep the door closed, old girl. Don't let it affect you again.*

Rian huffs a dark laugh. "I've already set her plans into disarray. She can tell you about it on our next visit."

"I look forward to that," Demara says, smiling slightly. "I can only hope my marriage is as full of the love you've regaled us all with stories of."

Rian shoots me a look before addressing Demara once more. "We should be on our way, my queen. Sorcha and I wouldn't want to keep you from any other adoring fans."

Demara's laughter tinkles like a bell in the tense atmosphere. "You're right," she declares, clapping her hands together. "See that they're taken to the records room and given full access. And be sure to find them appropriate finery for the evening," Demara instructs the guards in the hall, her gaze lingering on me for an extra heartbeat before she pivots on her heel and vanishes back into the shadows.

Chapter 8

THE SOLDIERS, SILENT SPECTERS again in their crimson and ebony uniforms, escort us through a labyrinth of corridors with such efficiency that we have no chance to speak. Not that I know what to say, after that emotional escapade. I'm still reeling from the constant back-and-forth with Rian, from his teasing to his veiled attempts at pushing me toward what he seems so certain is the answer to the Oracle's riddle, coupled with a day in the damned dungeons.

We're taken to the records room, a cavernous chamber lined floor-to-ceiling with metal shelves filled with dusty scrolls and leather-bound tomes. A magical fire crackles in the hearth, its glow a welcome reprieve from the dungeon's gloom. But it isn't warm enough. The chill of the dungeons clings to me.

"We'll return in one hour," the one called Raken says. They leave us alone, the heavy door closing with a resounding finality, leaving me and Rian alone in the vast room.

As soon as the door shuts, I bring forth my lights, letting the magic warm me.

"Are you well?" Rian asks, turning to face me. The flickering faelight from my will-o'-the-wisps dances across his features, giving him an almost ethereal glow. "Are you still upset with me?"

"I'm fine," I manage as I pace the room, my fingertips grazing on the scrolls just to not have to look at Rian. You don't blame the child for scribbling on the walls when you gave him the ink pens. He didn't likely mean to unsettle me with his talk of 'completion' and waiting for his queen. Not any more than he usually does, that is. "I simply... didn't expect to go from prisoner to party guest in a breath."

"Demara enjoys her games as much as I do," he says, his voice nonchalant as always. I resist the urge to roll my eyes. *Wasn't he just chastised by the Oracle for this?*

The reminder of the Oracle sharpens my focus, and I turn my attention to the rows of shelves. If we're lucky, there's something in this room that can help us better understand the riddle. I waste no time and begin scanning the titles, pulling down volumes with care. Rian follows me, as expected, his steps slow and deliberate, as though we have all the time in the world.

"You truly believe you'll find something here, Sorcha?" he asks after a few moments, his voice filled with skepticism. "Their magic isn't ours, remember. You're chasing shadows. Better to chase me," he says slyly.

"I'm not looking for a spell," I mutter, flipping through a thick, leather-bound tome. "I'm trying to understand what the Oracle meant when she claimed we needed completion. There *must* be more to it."

Rian's lips curl into a familiar smirk as he leans against a nearby shelf, watching me. "I'm certain there's much more to it. An entire evening's worth, in fact. Under the sheets, perhaps?"

I stop mid-page, my fingers curling tightly around the edges of the leaflet. I can feel the pressure building, the weight of the cuffs, the constant pull of the chain connecting us, the suffocating presence of his words. It's more than just frustration now. His constant innuendos, the sly remarks: they're pushing me toward a fear that he might be right. After all, is sex not binding in some way, a coming together? Did I not accidentally ask for this?

"Perhaps this ball will clear our heads," Rian suggests, pushing himself off the shelf and walking toward me. "Sometimes, thinking less helps us find the answers. Sometimes, it's better to be in the moment." His hand reaches out to tilt my chin up, forcing me to meet his gaze.

I shoot him a withering glare. My patience wears thinner with every word out of his mouth. And I don't want to admit it, but what if the Oracle's riddle *is* that simple? What if I have to... give myself to Rian to find the answer, to remove the cuffs? Had my half-hearted wish set a course that I'd never intended to follow? The thought claws at me, a combination of dread and the unsettling possibility that this might be the only way.

His eyes are piercing, intense, but I break the connection, pulling back instinctively. "I need to find something concrete," I insist, turning back to the shelf and pulling down another volume, my fingers trembling. But nothing in the room gives me any further insight.

"There must be another way," I repeat. "The Oracle's words—*completion*—they don't have to mean..."

"Me?" Rian finishes for me, his tone cooling, like a mask slipping into place. His teasing fades, replaced by something sharper, more deliberate. "You think there's some grand answer hidden in these pages that will magically solve everything? You're chasing illusions, Sorcha. And I know illusions."

His words feel different this time, less like banter and more like a negotiation. He watches me carefully, as though weighing every move I make. The playful smirk is still there, but there's a calculation behind it now—he's always been able to read me better than I'd like, but now it seems transactional. Like he's waiting for me to give in, to accept his terms.

I hesitate, and for a moment, the idea of giving in feels... inevitable. Maybe this is all part of the wish I set into action. Maybe he's always known it would come to this—a matter of timing, of patience, of letting me run myself ragged until I have no choice but to relent and free him. Free him by giving away even more of myself.

I clench my jaw, flipping through the pages, but before I can respond, the door to the records room creaks open, and Raken steps inside, his crimson and ebony uniform a stark contrast to the flickering magic light.

"Your hour is up," he says, his voice formal. "The Queen is expecting you to prepare for the ball."

I exhale, releasing my tight grip on the book. The weight of the moment slips away, but only temporarily. There's no escaping this—at some point, the decision will be made, whether by me or by the circumstances closing in around us. If nothing else, I can tell myself I tried to find an alternative.

We follow the guards through the winding halls until we arrive at a chamber swathed in tapestries that whisper of ancient battles and loves lost to time. The large four-poster bed, one we'll certainly need to share, is draped in luxurious velvet curtains, and the windows are covered with elaborate silk drapes. A grand fireplace crackles with yet another cool magical fire.

The other guard, whose name I still don't know, holds out a swath of fabric. "For you, crown prince and guest," he rumbles, laying out the clothes on the bed. "The party begins promptly. Please dress and join us immediately in the ballroom." He inclines his head and exits, Raken following behind him.

Rian shrugs out of his jacket and unbuttons his shirt. The fabric flutters to the ground in pieces, a reminder of his illusion magic at work. The muscles of his back shift beneath his skin with each movement, the black of his tattoo undulating. He looks around the room, a luxurious vision of vampire hospitality. "We will have time to come together after the party. This place is as good as any."

"Of course," I say, my voice a faint murmur. All the difficulties of the dungeon, of the Oracle's riddle, have wrung me out. I simply need to get through this evening, complete the wish, and get out of Rian's presence.

I pick up the gown meant for me. It's a confection of midnight blue, the fabric shimmering like the night sky, trimmed with delicate silver embroidery. The color of Rian's eyes. I swallow back the scowl threatening to rise.

"Sorcha," Rian calls, and I turn to find him transformed. Gone is the roguish rake; in his place stands a man who can command the attention of a court. His suit was white as the moon, a contrast to his dark hair, and it made the blue of his eyes startlingly vivid. "Shall I help you?"

I nod, ever frustrated that I can't even dress myself without Rian as my shirt catches along the chain.

"You no longer hide yourself from me," he says quietly, his eyes dragging over the softness of my stomach, the thatched stretch marks over my pale skin and the jagged scar from Jackson.

"You've already seen it," I reply, turning my back to him as we slip the dress over my head. His magic allows it to flit into place over the cuffs and he deftly fastens the delicate silver cords that criss-cross my back. The sensation of his warm breath against my skin threatens to light a fire of desire within me, and I force it down. But with the dress on, it's like I donned my armor. Protection to get me through tonight and through this wish.

"Ready?" he asks, his voice carrying a note of challenge.

"Ready," I confirm, drawing a steadying breath. For the ball, for whatever completion may mean, and perhaps, finally, for whatever choice I must make next.

Chapter
9

As Rian guides me through the crowd, his hand resting firmly on my back, I take in all the grandeur surrounding us. The ballroom is a sea of vibrant colors, silk gowns, and shimmering jewels, all swirling together under the glow of chandeliers that cast a golden hue over the festivities. The scent of roses intertwines with the heady aroma of iron in the air, creating a unique and intoxicating scent that permeates the room.

My gown, the embroidered designs catching the light like stars, trails behind me as we move towards the dance floor. The lights are stunning, like our firefly and will-o'-the-wisp faelights but... colder. Everything is colder here. I wonder why.

"It's the electricity, but a more fused type," Rian murmurs into my ear as we circle the room. "Something newfangled from the humans that Demara and her council have adapted."

I grab a drink from a passing server, a chilled glass of deep red liquid. A quick sniff tells me it's fruit wine. "I didn't ask about the lights," I say, my voice clipped. "I wondered about the cold. And to be completely literal, I didn't ask or wish anything at all."

He leans in, his lips dragging over the curve of my ear. "You desired it in your mind, framed it as a demand, all the while I could hear it."

I restrain a shiver and put a little distance from us, gulping my fruit wine. "And that it was about the *cold*?"

"I'm allowed a little... leeway in interpreting the wishes I grant," he says, brandishing a devastatingly handsome smile. But the limitations he claimed in the woods implied the opposite.

Rather than try to understand another of his games, I roll my eyes and toss back the rest of the wine before handing the empty glass to him. Just as I do, Phaeron, clad in a midnight black uniform, appears across the room. His blond hair gleams golden in the lamplight, and he moves toward me with purpose. A frown flickers across the face of a pretty blonde woman watching him, but she disappears into the crowd before I can linger on the thought.

"Will you honor me with a dance, Lady Sorcha?" Phaeron asks, his obsidian gaze locking onto mine.

I glance down at the chain that connects me to Rian, lifting it with a sardonic smile. "If you can navigate my deadweight."

"Can't be more than a few feet away, can I?" Rian retorts with a hint of annoyance.

Phaeron's smile is indulgent. "I'll manage your chain, Sorcha. We'll remain close. It will be more... intimate that way," he says, his voice a smooth caress.

Rian grudgingly stretches his cuffed arm and offers a theatrical smile. "This is as far as you can go. Do try not to drag me around too much, Phaeron."

Phaeron simply raises an eyebrow and turns back to me, extending his hand once again. "Shall we dance?"

I hesitate for a moment before gingerly placing my free hand in his outstretched one. "Why not?"

We take to the floor, the chain between me and Rian limiting our movements, keeping us near him as he watches, frowning slightly. Phaeron's touch is cool, the chill of his skin seeping through the fabric of my gown. His grip tightens as we sway in a confined space, just as he promised, intimate and calculated.

"I apologize for the earlier incident," Phaeron murmurs, never taking his eyes from mine. "I did not know you weren't aware it was a jest and thought it was real—"

I'm quick to reassure him. "It's fine, Phaeron. It wasn't your fault."

"I suppose I should have known this wasn't a usual visit for Rian." His hands close in on my waist and hip, bringing me closer to him. With Rian forcing me to remain in place, it is as intimate as Phaeron had claimed. We can't do more than sway.

"The cuffs didn't give you a hint?" I reply dryly.

"That and that he wasn't with Isabel," he says with a smirk, revealing the faintest hint of fangs. "All his diplomatic visits are usually accompanied by her."

Right. The mention of Isabel's name is a cold draft in the already frigid temperature of the room. "Yes, this is different," I manage. "We were attempting to unbind ourselves."

His dark eyes flick towards my wrist and the chain hovering taut towards Rian. "What happened there?" he asks, the question mild.

I hesitate but decide to tell him the truth. If the Oracle's riddle has roots in the vampire court, perhaps Phaeron's insight could help me unravel it faster. "There was a wish," I begin, glancing over at Rian. "A misbegotten wish. Half-hearted, but literally, binding."

"Tell me more," Phaeron says, his eyes gleaming with intrigue. "Perhaps I can help."

I slide my gaze over the busy ballroom, the dancers spinning around us. "Can you keep a secret?"

He leans in. "Fuil is the soul of discretion, Lady Sorcha. Nothing discovered here will leave these walls without Demara's permission."

I frown slightly. That protection only lasts as long as Demara keeps it a secret, if she uses the knowledge as a retaliation in her game with Rian. I take a heavy breath. At least if I explain it, there won't be unfounded rumors going around.

I tell Phaeron everything, taking up most of the song with my tale. "And even though the spell didn't work," I finish, "it seems my supposed wish was granted."

"And you thought something like 'I'd give anything to be bound to Rian?'" he asks, his tone gentle but probing.

My cheeks flush at the reminder of my foolishness. "Yes, but it wasn't meant to be—"

"No need to explain yourself to me, my lady. I can see the pain in your eyes. You wished for the freedom to choose. Rian has that freedom. Ironic that you bound yourself further."

I falter in my steps, surprised by the unique insight, but he steadies me effortlessly. I make a soft, somewhat agreeing noise, hoping that's enough of an answer. I can't say that was what I wished for, as it's more likely a silly manifestation of past Sorcha's desires.

He watches me for a moment before continuing, his voice low and persuasive. "The Oracle said to complete it, you must find what lies at the heart of your bond. Have you considered that you gave him something to receive the wish? You'd have given anything to be bound, and now you are. Whatever you gave is the heart of your bond. And you simply need to take it back to unbind it. Would that not complete it?"

I consider the thought, staring over Phaeron's shoulders at Rian. He stands apart from the dancers, only a few feet away, his gaze fixed on me with an intensity that speaks volumes. "But what have I given him?" I ask, my voice nearly a whisper. I've done all I could not to give him more of me—of time, my attention, my—my heart.

"You've given him power over you," Phaeton suggests, sounding almost casual. "And now you must take it back."

I scowl at him, and his arms tighten around me protectively.

"I mean no offense, Sorcha," Phaeron adds quietly, leaning close enough that his breath teases stray strands of my hair. "But you have. And you must take it back."

He attempts to turn us towards the livelier throng of dancers. But my chain holds us back, staying out the outskirts of the dance floor. A metaphor for sure.

"Take back the power I've given him?" I let out a breath. "How?"

He smiles, his gaze lingering on me. "Dancing with me is a start. It's a minor act of defiance, but it's something. Every step away from him, even if only for a moment, is a step toward reclaiming yourself."

"Lucky I said yes then," I reply, flashing a small smile at him.

"Indeed," he agrees, his voice low and persuasive. "And there's more. You could break free from more than just this bond, Sorcha. There are other ways to gain power." He leans closer, his next words a whisper. "You could stay here. In Fuil. I would turn you if you wish."

My brows raise in surprise. "Turn me? Into a vampire?"

"Yes," he says, his gaze never wavering. "You would retain your fae essence, but gain the strength and immortality of the Turned. Your magic would remain."

"It isn't much to speak of," I say, almost idly. The weight of the offer hits me like an icy wave, laced with equal parts fear and fascination.

"Raken told me of your faelights," Phaeron says, a white-blond brow raising. "Enough of us are mired in the past that the Queen's human lights aren't as popular as they could be. Your magical flame? Something warm for our undead veins? You could live here quite comfortably if you bottled and sold them."

My own brows raise in response at the thought. Even with all my whining about leaving Avalaruin to avoid a permanent binding, I'd never actually considered what I'd do here. The idea of severing ties with Avalaruin, of living an entirely different life, of my magic actually having meaning for once... it's tempting.

But the vampires have their own rules, their own power, but it's a life of limitations, much like the fae's betrothal lists. And then there's the treaty...

"The treaty forbids you from turning others," I say, the words slipping out as my mind races.

"The treaty forbids vampires from transforming *humans* without council approval," he leans in closer, his breath hot against my neck. "Not fae."

My heart quickens as the implications of his words cascade through me. "I'd never even considered…" I trail off.

"You would be free of the constraints of your world," he explains, his voice full of promise, "and you would be powerful in ours. We would offer you a place in this court."

"But why? Why offer that to me?"

"It sounds as though you need a fresh start. To remove yourself from the bonds of your past," he says, looking wistful. "It would be my honor to give that to you."

It's everything I thought I wanted—an escape from Avalanin, from the endless expectations, from the binding lists and a life without control. But becoming a Turned vampire—one who can never experience the sun—is another form of bondage, just wrapped in different rules. It's no choice, when it is merely for escape.

I glance at Rian again. His eyes are still on me, watching, waiting. He's as much a part of this equation as Phaeron. The Oracle's riddle hangs over us all, but one truth becomes clear: I've already given Rian more power than I should have. Becoming a vampire wouldn't free me—it would just replace one bond with another.

I gently push away from Phaeron, needing some space to gather my thoughts and catch my breath. Not from physical exhaustion—we've only been swaying to the music—but from the possible revelations brought forth by our conversation.

Phaeron's hand steadies me, his touch firm yet gentle. "I simply ask that you consider it."

I nod, mind still reeling. "Thank you."

The melody starts again, soft and low before building into a faster waltz, sweeping through the pillars and over the sea of twirling gowns like a gust of wind. Rian steps towards me.

"Sorcha," Phaeron's voice draws me back to him as he extends his hand again. "Have I overwhelmed you so that you must return to your jailer, or will you allow me another dance?"

"I—"

"Just a dance," he says, one corner of his mouth ticking up. "Giving you a *little* more power."

"A favor to me then?" I ask, rather bitterly. I'm beginning to tire of men attempting to 'help' me.

"A double benefit," Phaeron says. "As I have you in my arms again."

My hackles settle and I nearly slump my shoulders. I'm too quick to distrust, and Phaeron has done nothing to earn my cynicism. *Except the dungeon*, my worst impulses remind me. I quickly shake the thought away. "I don't believe I can manage this piece, Phaeron. We can't complete the steps."

"Let me assist," Rian says, stepping closer to us. His hands find their way onto Phaeron's broad shoulders, a gesture both intimate and bold.

Phaeron casts a glance behind him at Rian, a silent exchange passing between them—an accord struck in a heartbeat. I watch, fascinated, as Rian gives a slight nod, signaling his readiness to act as Phaeron's double in this peculiar arrangement. Phaeron extends his hand again, and I accept, placing my fingers into his.

As the music quickens, Phaeron leads me into the waltz, our steps falling into the rapid tempo with surprising ease. Rian moves in tandem behind him, his guiding touch on Phaeron's shoulders steering us across the floor. My skirts billow around us as the waltz commands us to be faster, more daring, and we comply, our footsteps a drumbeat against the marble floor. I can feel the heat of their twin gazes. When I look up, my eyes won't stop drifting to Rian's and I have to force myself to focus on Phaeron instead. My gaze can't be trusted and so I close my eyes and let them lead me instead.

We twirl and dip, the world blurring into a tapestry of light and sound, every note of the waltz a pulse that beats in time with my racing heart. Phaeron leads with the precision of a skilled swordsman, every step executed with poise and confidence. Yet it's Rian's subtle guidance that infuses each motion with an undercurrent of passion and control. The sensation of being danced by two men at once—though only one truly holds me—is exhilarating.

Behind them, Queen Demara ascends the dais. The musicians' hands still on their instruments, the music lingering and then fading into silence. Phaeron releases me, stepping away from Rian. His full lips are quirked in a small frown and I wonder why.

"Remember my offer," he whispers in my ear, kissing me lightly on the cheek before striding gracefully to join his queen, not looking back.

"Esteemed guests," Demara begins, her voice like a soft chime of crystal. "The time has come for me to entertain the company of my suitors."

Rian moves to stand beside me. "What did Phaeron offer?" he asks idly, but beneath his tone is edged with steel.

Queen Demara's suitors begin their approach, a petite woman in a vibrant red gown introducing them one by one.

"Nothing," I whisper back, but as the room focuses on the spectacle before us, my eyes are drawn to Rian. I had given him power over me, for decades. My twentieth year put that to bed.

How have I given him power over me now?

I WAS EIGHTEEN YEARS old.

The grand hall was alive with light and magic as the fae gathered for another Beltane celebration. The chandeliers glowed with enchanted fireflies, creating a glow over the tiled room. Fae of all ages mingled, their laughter and chatter creating a joyful buzz in the air. I adjusted the shimmering emerald gown I wore, feeling a mix of excitement and nervousness. Tonight, I had one wish, a desire that had been building inside me for years.

I still wanted Rian; I'd just become more... realistic about it.

At twenty years old, *he* was now eligible for the Beltane binding rites, though most believed he wouldn't take part for many more years. As the crown prince, he didn't have the chances the rest of us did. Once he binds, it was for good. However, his father's declining health could change things, and I didn't want to miss my chance with him. I had wished, over and over, that he would be the one to take my virginity. To give me one night. Just once. That was all I wanted before he inevitably chose Isabel, or Carol, or Margarite, or any of the other eligible women who would fit beside him as queen. *Let me have that one moment, something of my own.*

I scanned the room, my eyes landing on Rian near the center of the ballroom, looking regal and composed in his dark suit. His dark hair was wild and loose, down to his mid back now, and his blue eyes seemed to catch the light, making them appear even more striking. My heart skipped a beat as I watched him, the years of longing and unspoken love swirling inside me.

But he wasn't alone. As always, Isabel stood by his side, stunning in a form-fitting red gown that hugged her curves perfectly. Her flowing auburn hair fell in soft waves past her shoulders. A frown creased my brow as I realized that no matter how much I wished for Rian's attention, Isabel always seemed to steal it away.

Taking a deep breath, I mustered up my courage and made my way through the crowd towards Rian. This was my last chance, after all. As I approached, our eyes met for a moment and I hoped he had heard my wish. But then Isabel leaned in, whispering something in his ear, and his attention shifted back to her.

"Rian," I called out, unwilling to let a little difficulty stop me from getting my wish. My voice cut through the noise of the party, causing a few conversations to pause.

He looked up, surprise flickering across his face. "Sorcha," he said with a polite but distant tone. "You look beautiful tonight."

"Thank you," I replied softly. "I was hoping we could talk."

Isabel's narrowed eyes and tight smile revealed her displeasure at my presence, but she maintained a facade of pleasantness. "I'm sure Rian will find you another time, Sorcha. He's quite busy tonight."

I forced a smile. "Rian can tell me that himself, Isabel."

But Rian, ever the diplomat, intervened with a charming smile. "Sorcha, I'd be delighted to speak with you later this evening. I'll come to you when that time arrives." His firm tone brooked no argument.

I tried to hide my disappointment, my brewing pain. "Of course. I understand."

I turned away, the weight of my unfulfilled wish pressing down on me. I had wanted so badly to be with Rian, to share something special with him. Despite how much I wished, he remained just out of reach.

I wandered through the ballroom in a daze, watching as Rian and Isabel moved through the crowd together, always close. I tried to mingle, distracting myself with conversations and laughter, but my mind kept drifting back to Rian.

As the night wore on, I found myself standing near the edge of the ballroom again, watching him from afar. He still looked handsome and composed, but now there was a tension in his posture that I couldn't quite understand. Isabel's hand rested possessively on his arm as they mingled with other fae. And despite my efforts to keep a positive mindset, it seemed like I had missed my chance with Rian. But I wasn't giving up that easily. Maybe, just maybe, my wish could still come true.

I wished, with all my heart, with all I had, that he would hear, that he would understand how much I cared, that he would give me his time, that he would have me for this night. Then I'd leave, let Isabel and the others have him.

But he remained distant, his attention focused on Isabel. I felt my heart hardening, the years of unrequited love and longing turning into something colder, something more resigned.

As the night drew to a close, I stepped outside for air. The garden was cloaked in darkness, save for the gentle glow of moonlight peeking through the trees. The only sound was the soft rustling of leaves in the breeze, creating an almost ethereal atmosphere. I leaned against a towering marble column, staring up at the twinkling stars above. The cool night air brushed against my skin.

A sudden tear slid down my cheek, but I quickly brushed it away. I couldn't let anyone see my vulnerability. It was me against the world, and I had to stay strong. But as I gazed up at the endless expanse of stars, I felt small and insignificant in comparison. Just Sorcha, just a nobody.

Suddenly, a voice cut through the quiet garden. "Sorcha."

I turned at the sound. Rian stood a few feet away, his expression unreadable.

"Rian," I breathed, my voice trembling with emotion. "I... Hi." I forced a smile, inwardly cringing at how awkward I sounded.

"I'm sorry I've been distant," he said, stepping closer. "It's just... there's so much going on."

That excuse sounded familiar, but I pushed it away.

"I understand," I replied, trying to keep my voice steady. "I just wanted to be there for you."

He reached out, his hand brushing against my cheek. "I know, darl—Sorcha. And I appreciate it. More than you know."

I wanted to pour my heart out to him, to tell him everything that was bubbling inside me. But fear held me back, fear of rejection and losing what little connection we had.

Instead, I offered him my wish again, silently pleading with all my heart that he would hear it this time. *Please, Rian, please. Just once. Just be with me once. Then never again will I ask.*

But his expression shuttered, and a frown creased his lips. "Sorcha, I—"

"Rian!" Isabel's voice pierced the night like a knife, sharp and urgent. "There you are. We need to go. The elder meeting is beginning."

Rian pulled back, a look of frustration crossing his face. "I'm terribly sorry, Sorcha. I must go."

I nodded, feeling like my heart was breaking all over again. "Of course. Go."

He hesitated, seeming to regret his abrupt departure. "I'll speak with you later. When I'm free. I promise."

I watched as he walked away, Isabel's hand slipping into his as they disappeared into the darkness. My wish for Rian had remained unfulfilled yet again, and it felt like he was slipping further and further away from me.

A coldness settled over my heart as I wiped away my tears and turned back towards the ballroom. The night was still young, and I had a life to live. I only hoped Rian would catch up.

Pity it took me so much time to follow through.

WITH SUDDEN CLARITY AND determination, I grasp his hand and pull him away from the ballroom. He follows wordlessly, and the colorful blur of faces and sounds fades into the background as we reappear in the deserted corridor. The only sound now is our hurried footsteps and the pounding of my heart.

"Where are we going?" he asks, his voice a low rumble that vibrates through the chaos of my thoughts.

Golden chandeliers drip with crystals above us, casting prismatic shadows that dance like faeries on the walls. Their light washes over Rian's features, painting him into a vision of shadow and light.

"To our rooms, Rian." I gesture to the door ahead of us, its heavy frame blocking what lies beyond. With each second that passes, the anticipation builds—a crescendo of possibilities that could either bind me tighter to him or set us free.

His eyes search mine. "For our completion?"

"For completion."

Chapter 10

IF PHAERON HAS IT right, if the heart of my bond with Rian may involve his power over me, then everything about this encounter must be about me, and my power. Whatever I can cobble together this night.

As I magick my faelights into the fireplace, Rian slips the white jacket from his shoulders, a small smile appearing on his lips. "Any preferences, love?" he asks as he drops it to the ground, the now-ripped fabric whispering against itself as it falls. "I've a list of them myself."

I swallow, my pulse pounding. This is my first test, my first chance to break the pattern of yielding to him, of waiting on his whims. Every turning point between us has been his design: his hand extending friendship when I wished for a companion, his acceptance of these handcuffs. But this time, the decision is mine.

"Undress me," I say, pushing a firmness into my voice that I hope hides any hint of hesitation.

His eyes light up with a quiet thrill, but his approach is slow, almost reverent. Long fingers brush against the fabric of my dress, his touch light as he undoes the intricate laces that hold it together.

Each pull feels like a soft caress, igniting anticipation like a fire coiling within me. I close my eyes, savoring the sensation, grounding myself in this choice—*my* choice, this time. Whatever this wish demands, I refuse to let it bind me further. Tonight, this moment is mine.

The final lace slips free, and my gown pools around my ankles. I stand before him, bathed in the flickering light of the hearth, and his eyes roam over me, a mixture of awe and hunger transforming his face, as if I were the most beautiful creature he'd ever laid eyes upon—damn the stretch marks, damn the scars—and in that instant, I want to believe him.

Control, I remind myself, the word a steady rhythm against the rush of my heartbeat. *Don't lose it.*

Without breaking his gaze, I step backward toward the bed, and, as if bound by more than the chain, Rian follows. He's moving in rhythm with me, point and counterpoint, a dance I'm determined to lead. There's something in his eyes: a pull that's more than just the cuff linking us, a ravenous and unrestrained desire.

When the back of my legs hit the edge of the bed, I sink onto the mattress, holding his gaze as he sheds his shirt, dropping it to the floor. Sliding back toward the headboard, I watch as he crawls onto the bed, his movements a smooth, prowling grace. The velvet curtains pool around us dark as midnight, enveloping us in their shadow while the silk sheets glide against my skin as he hovers above me, his breath mingling with mine in the space between us. The earthy scent of him infuses the air as the strands of his long hair brush against my shoulders, my neck.

The tip of his nose grazes my cheek, the slightest touch that amplifies the arousal already pooling within my core. "Tell me what you want," he murmurs, his voice a deep whisper that coils through the room. It reminds me of our moment at the first inn, but it's different now. This isn't a command; it's an invitation, a plea.

"I want you," I whisper, a confession my clear-head will rue my lust-filled mind making.

I'll rationalize it later: I want him because he's gorgeous, I want him because he's here, I want him because it's the only way to remove the cuffs. Craving, convenience, or completion, whatever will protect myself.

This isn't about him. It's about my choice.

His hand reaches out to cradle my cheek, his touch gentle yet possessive. "Then have me," he breathes, brushing his lips against mine in a feather-light kiss.

I respond, skimming my lips over his silken mouth. His tongue softly presses against the seam of my lips before dipping into the heat of my mouth. The rigidity in my spine fades away as he deepens the kiss, his hands tangling in my unruly hair as he pulls me closer. My arms wrap tightly around his neck, my body responding to his with a desperate need and longing that I can't keep suppressed. I try to close myself off from him, but it's impossible when he's so close, so real.

Rian's lips leave mine, trailing a path of fire down my neck. "Sorcha," he murmurs against the skin of my collarbone, the vulnerable dip of my throat, his voice husky with need. I tilt my head back, giving him access to every inch of my exposed throat. "Darling, yes." There's a desperation in his voice I'd never heard before, he sounds nearly crazed as he rumbles against my skin. "Give your-self to me. Let me have you, at last. Entirely."

The words break through the haze, letting me remember where I am, what we're doing. Rian doesn't notice, lips sucking a mark into the space under my ear, his hands pressed into the mattress above my head, his body boxing me in. I can't let that continue, I can't let him take *me*. With a surge of strength, I shift, flipping us so I'm straddling him, a rush of triumph warming my veins as I pin him beneath me. His look of surprise only fans the fire burning within me, his hands hovering over my hips, caught between instinct and caution.

But I know exactly what I want. And for once, I am determined to take it. My power, my wish. My damned bond. I am the one in control now, that this moment is about my pleasure and my power.

"Touch me," I demand. Another memory of our time at the inn, only days ago, threatens to rise but I force it down. This isn't about a wish, or a transaction. It's a decision—*my* decision.

Rian's hands roam over my body, dragging over every curve and dip. My waist, my spine, my breasts, never lingering too long in one place. I arch my back, inviting him closer and he sits up, enfolding me in his arms. His mouth follows the trail his hands took, over my neck, down to my breasts, as far as he can reach. The heat of his breath sends sparks cascading down my spine and I clutch at his shoulders to steady myself, stroking over the defined muscles there and over his back, lines of pink appearing under my nails, marks to memorialize my short time with him. My thighs tighten around his hips, and I can feel every inch of him through the thin barrier of fabric that still clings to him.

I take control again, guiding his hand lower, where my need is sharpest. His fingers tease at my body, rubbing gently against my core. My breath comes in shallow gasps as I grind against his hand, seeking the release that's tantalizingly close. His gaze skims over me and a flash of insecurity threatens to rise, imagining how many other women have been in this position, how often his eyes tripped over Isabel's perfect form, instead of the jiggles and rolls my body creates as I move.

But all doubt drowns as he growls, a low, feral sound that makes my heart stutter and my body clench in anticipation.

"Show me," he nearly snarls. "Let me see you undone."

I stop comparing, stop *thinking* and instead seek the pleasure building within me.

"More," I moan, my voice a breathless whisper as the fire within me starts to burn brighter. "I want more."

He complies, dipping low to suck a mark into my breast, working his fingers as the feeling rises higher and higher. I roll my hips, thighs squeezing, back arching, holding his head to my breast until I'm dragged over the edge, a sensation that's quick and sharp. But my body doesn't relax, it's a bow that's been prepared, warmed-up for the ultimate performance. That was the appetizer, the climax to clear my head before the meal I plan on making of Rian.

He presses one more soft kiss into my skin before lifting his head. His eyes, normally so blue, are dark as night, eclipsed by desire. "Still more, darling?"

With a growl of my own, I reach between us, fingers deft as I undo the laces of his trousers and release him. He sucks in a breath, his hands clutching my shoulders as I sink down on him, burying him within me inch by inch. I don't let either of us adjust before lifting and crashing back into him hard enough that I know I'll feel the imprint of him days later.

He groans, sliding his grip down past the softness of my stomach to my thick waist. His gaze travels from the space where we're joined up to my eyes. There's something raw there, a need I fear may be reflected in my own eyes, something I don't want to be reminded of. My hands find his face, the cuff clinking against the heat of his jaw, as I draw his lips down. He buries his face into my neck, his lips against the edge of my collarbone, sucking and biting and licking while I continue rising and falling against him, the jingle of the chain a rhythm of our coupling.

Our breaths come quicker, his teeth dragging against the juncture of my shoulder as I press my mouth into his hair. He mutters nonsensical words against my skin—ones I'll try not to remember in the stark morning light—how good it feels, how much he wants me. Things lust brings forth that reality will wash away. Closing my eyes, I breathe in the scent of him, to remember, to savor, to remind me of this one moment where I got what I wanted. Where I had control, power, for once.

Each push away from his body brings an emptiness that only he can fill, each pull down a fullness that makes me feel alive and whole. He thrusts up into me, erratic and sharp, fingertips pressing bruises into the soft skin at my thighs, as he roars his completion. The sound melds into the rush of blood in my ears and the thunderous pleasure rolling through my body. Light bursts from the hearth, my faelights exploding into sparks that flash around us, a dancing firestorm to culminate our joining.

And the cuffs remain in place.

THERE'S ALWAYS BEEN A moment, after intimacy, when I should be basking in the languid relaxation that settles into my muscles, the slow ebb of my pulse, and that soft feeling of release. But I've never reacted that way. Instead, I always end up feeling exposed, my skin raw and vulnerable.

Now, though? In the aftermath of our so-called "completion," lying here on cool, wrinkled sheets, my skin still tingling from the shared warmth, I almost experience that elusive calm.

Rian shifts beside me, his hand brushing lightly over the cuff still fastened to my wrist. His brow furrows, and he lets out a faint sigh as he glances down at the unbroken chain between us. And there's a flicker of disappointment—slight but unmistakable—that hits me deep in my gut.

There's that vulnerability I'm used to. So much for feeling powerful, for claiming this moment as mine.

Rian smirks, but there's something sharp behind it as he runs his fingers along my bare shoulder. "Well," he says, voice light but holding a hint of suggestion, "perhaps it just takes... more than once to *complete* the task."

"You'd like that," I mutter under my breath, even as heat rises to my cheeks. The cuffs' stubborn grip nags at me, like an unwanted reminder of how far I've let him into my life, and now my body.

It wasn't a question, but Rian answers anyway with a wolfish grin forming on his lips. "Yes," he says confidently, his eyes sparkling with desire. "I've yet to have you under me, darling. I've yet to *see* you experience true bliss. Although I did enjoy the view I had." He leans in close, his warm breath caressing my lips as he speaks. "Our bond remains incomplete."

My resolve wavers when his lips brush against mine in a tentative kiss, but I turn away, letting his lips drag against my cheek instead.

"*Repetition* isn't the answer," I say, forcing myself to meet his gaze and keep my walls firmly in place.

He shifts, his thumb grazing my cheek as his eyes soften with something almost tender. "I'm only suggesting... maybe there are other ways. Other types of completion." His voice carries a strange mix of playfulness and an edge of desperation that gives me pause.

But I push it down, heaving a sigh and hoping the gesture hides any of my sudden discomfort. "We need to try another path. If there's an answer, it's out there, *not* in this room." I push up on my elbow, but before I can say more, a knock at the door breaks the tension, sparing us both from whatever argument was waiting to erupt.

"Master Rian," a muffled voice calls from the other side. "A message from Avalaruin. The council requires your presence."

Rian's expression shifts, the hunger in his eyes cooling, replaced by something unreadable. He doesn't look surprised; if anything, he seems resigned.

"Well," he murmurs, his tone almost playful, like he's sharing a private joke, "it seems we're needed back sooner than I'd expected." He pulls the sheet higher around our shoulders, his arm slipping around my waist. "Perhaps we linger a little longer? One last moment of peace before duty calls?"

I tense under his arm, shifting away. The thought of being paraded before the council, cuffs and all, makes my stomach twist uncomfortably. This wasn't supposed to happen—being dragged into Avalaruin with Rian still bound to me like this. "We can't go back like this," I mutter, pushing myself up on one elbow. "We must fix it first. We could go back to the records room, search for a spell, or even return to the Oracle. Anything to avoid... this," I gesture between us, "being put on display."

Rian's gaze sharpens, humor slipping away. "Trust me, Sorcha. If the council is calling, it's urgent. We can't afford any detours."

I open my mouth to protest, to insist that a few more hours could give us the answers we need. After all, he was fine dallying here when it meant remaining in bed, and the minute it isn't his idea, we leave? But he's already sitting up, running a hand through his disheveled hair.

"Thank you," he calls to the door, his tone a notch lower, more authoritative. He swings his legs over the side of the bed and stands, the sheet cascading to the floor. Unashamedly, he stretches, pulling the chain between us taut.

I watch him and the lean lines of his body silhouetted against the magical fire. There are scratch marks over his shoulders and back, pinkish lines that blend into the swirling tattoos on his skin. His hair, always wild, is matted and tangled, the strands twisted from my fingers. Once, the sight of him this way would have scattered every sensible thought from my mind. At least I now have an excellent memory to take into exile, because that's where I'm headed as soon as everyone realizes what I've done.

"We need to keep looking," I insist, trying to sound stern, pushing away the images from only an hour before. "And hide the cuffs."

Rian looks back at me, a ghost of his usual smirk appearing. "Of course, darling. Perhaps the same artifice we used in the streets of Fuil? A little... snuggling?"

The words stir something within me, a mix of irritation and something else, something I'm unwilling to name. "As long as no one finds out," I finally say.

His smile deepens, and I can see the glint of some hidden joke in his eyes. "Certainly not from me."

There's a trick in his face, but one I'm too wrung out to uncover. I sit up, the sheet slipping to my waist. His smile widens, predatory, as he holds out his hand. I hesitate, eyeing the cuff one last time, but then I take his hand, allowing him to pull me to my feet and to whatever consequences lie ahead.

Chapter

II

We depart Fuil immediately, tracing our path back on the boat over the crystal-clear waters of Prism Lake and onto Heriot Island. The alluring songs of the sirens no longer irritate me, my mind consumed with worries about returning to Avalaruin.

Just as it had before, when we slip through the cave on Heriot Island and return to Tixia Island, the world tilts. Instead of the dead of night, it is now a pleasant afternoon. And yet, I can barely stop shivering, though that could be the healthy dose of anxiety coursing through me. The warm sun beats down on our skin but provides little comfort as we make our way towards the Council House, each step fraught with nervous tension at whatever consequences may come when the elders see these stupid cuffs.

The grand hall of the Council House oozes an air of formality and importance, its high ceilings covered with intricate mosaics depicting scenes of ancient battles and mystical creatures. We walk upon polished marble floors, my heart racing with alarm as I know my secret is only hidden by the thin fabric of Rian's jacket. The weight of the cuffs seems even more stifling here, a reminder of the control I'm slowly losing.

The elders are already assembled in the chamber, their expressions a mix of curiosity and apathy as they eye us entering together. We squeeze onto one of the narrow benches, struggling to fit into the limited space. If I'm lucky, I'll fall off it and crack my head open. Anything to escape the judgment and mockery that will surely follow.

The presentation begins, some dull discussion about trade agreements. The elders don't notice me at first, and it only takes a few minutes to realize why.

Isabel is present, along with a handful of other heirs scattered throughout the room. Perhaps they mistake me as someone of importance, not looking closely enough to realize it's just Sorcha.

Rian sits beside me with a mask of calm on his face, politely nodding as one of the elder fae drones on about the price of steel. *Clearly of such importance that we needed to leave Fuil immediately.*

I try my best to look interested, mimicking the actions of Brennan, another heir we grew up with, as he listens attentively, nodding and making thoughtful expressions. But my acting skills are put to the ultimate test when Isabel shifts from her seat across the room and squeezes in beside me.

Already struggling to find room on the bench with just Rian and me, I now feel like I'm being swallowed whole as Isabel's body presses against mine. My arms and shoulders are crushed together to make space for a third body, my breasts nearly bursting up towards my neck. A bruise—made from Rian's lips—peeks from the edge of the fabric and I swallow the impulse to stare down at it.

"I didn't expect to see you here," Isabel says, her beautiful green eyes shining with curiosity. "Especially not in my usual seat."

Memories of years spent watching Rian gravitate towards Isabel flood my mind, causing bitterness to churn in my stomach. But I force myself not to care as I offer her a weak smile. "Yes, well, who among us isn't fascinated by dandelion trade values?"

Isabel lets out a laugh that rings through the air like music, revealing the long line of her rich umber neck, and catching the attention of the elders.

They pause in their presentation. Fintan, the elder in charge of courtship assignments, raises a bushy white eyebrow in our direction and I want nothing more than to sink into my seat and disappear. But I can't shift to hide, as even with how willowy Isabel is, she's solid and unmoving beside me. Instead, Rian clears his throat and redirects the elders' attention back to the presentation.

But he sneaks a hand onto my thigh. I squeak, surprised, and force myself quiet to avoid triggering another pause that will put too many eyes on me.

As the elders return to their conversations, Isabel leans in closer, her voice dropping to a conspiratorial whisper. "It seems you're quite... attached to Rian tonight."

I blanch, my eyes widening in fear as I glance down at our bound wrists and the glint of metal from the cuffs. *Did Rian tell her about our arrangement? Can she see the restraints?*

"Right..." I stammer, my mind frantically searching for an excuse. If Rian revealed our secret, it's simply more confirmation of my incompetence. And if he hasn't, there was no way I was going to confess anything to her.

Rian makes small circles with his fingers on my thigh, soothing and distracting at the same time.

Isabel's voice drops to a low whisper. "You know, Rian and I have a lot of history. Sometimes, it's simply about timing and understanding each other's roles in this world."

Confusion replaces my initial panic as I ask, "Roles? What do you mean?"

Isabel's eyes sparkle with an underlying edge as she replies, "You know. Some people are meant to be friends, others something more. It's all about finding the right... fit. Wouldn't you agree?"

I clench my teeth in frustration, my confusion quickly dissipating. She's asserting her claim over him, and she wants me to know it. Well, that's fine by me. *Just get these cursed cuffs off and I'll never darken either of your doors again.* If freedom were a wish, it would be one I'd grant without hesitation.

Beside me, Rian shifts, glancing at me, a flicker of something—hurt? disappointment?—crossing his gaze before he looks back to the elders. His hand remains on my thigh but goes still.

With forced nonchalance, I reply, "If something doesn't fit, one can always force it. It's often more fun that way." My smile is sharp as a dragon's tooth. Let her interpret the innuendo however she pleases.

Before Isabel can respond or twist the knife further, the head of the council clears his throat, drawing everyone's attention. "Prince Rian, your insights on the trade route would be appreciated."

Rian tilts his head in acknowledgement and speaks, his voice steady and authoritative. Isabel leans in again and I shake my head, pretending to be fully engrossed in the meeting. But as Rian speaks, his words blending with the soft murmurs of the elders, I steal a glance at Isabel.

Her eyes gleam with determination and a hint of challenge, as if daring me to contest her hold over Rian. But I don't want it. I want to take back whatever accidental connection we have. Rian can have the victory he asserted to the Oracle and they can continue their games without me as a pawn on their chessboard.

As the meeting drags on, my anxiety grows. I need to disappear, to hide from the curious glances and Isabel's knowing smile. But the cuffs keep me firmly in place.

Rian finishes his report, and the atmosphere in the chamber shifts. The elders nod in approval, their attention momentarily diverted from our clandestine connection. But life is unfair and before they move on to the next item on their agenda, an elder named Desmond (if memory serves) fixes me with a pointed stare.

"And why is Lady Sorcha present? She has no official role in these proceedings."

Rian is quick to reply, his voice cool and confident. "Sorcha is assisting me with a charm. Her presence is vital."

Desmond raises an eyebrow. "Sorcha? Assisting with a charm?"

There's a small titter through the room and I want to sink into the floor. *Yes, yes, we all know I'm bad at enchantments, no need to remind me.* But before I can think of a response, Fintan speaks up.

"Ah yes, Sorcha. I had not received a response to my letter. Do recall you have a courtship date tonight."

The terrible surprise hits me like an icy wave. Our impromptu trip to Fuil meant I received no messages from the council members. As sneakily as I can, I elbow Rian in the gut and he lets out a quiet grunt.

"Apologies for my delay, sir," I tell him, my tone as respectful as I can manage, given the circumstances and my own bitterness surrounding any future binding. "I'll... certainly be there." *Unless I bite my hand off to remove the cuffs and accept Phaeron's offer.*

"Yes, well. We hope it will be successful." He snaps, and a man scuttles over from a bench. "Brian is a scribe for Desmond, and a member of the illusion guild."

If nothing else, Brian is the definition of tall, dark, and handsome, but so is Rian. So was Noel. So was Elliot. That isn't an oddity among the fae.

Unlike the others, Brian's dark hair is styled in a neat bun, instead of wild and loose down his back. Also unlike the others is the soft paunch of his figure, similar to mine. He looks sweet and I see me trying to cook for us, destroying it (since following recipes are so similar to enchanting rituals), and the two of us fading away from starvation. Until he too, wants nothing to do with me and I might finally regain a smattering of freedom again. Still a long-suffering wife, but not a broodmare.

But I know better than to hope for such an outcome.

Rian's fingers claw against my thigh, sharp and possessive. I wince.

"I look forward to seeing you tonight, Brian," I tell him with a strained smile.

Fintan looks down his long nose at me. "Good luck, children. This is your last chance, after all."

The meeting finally ends. Isabel and Rian exchange a loaded glance. It looks as though they're communicating without words, lips silently moving until Rian finally shakes his head and Isabel nods sharply.

As the elders file out, Isabel leans in one last time, her voice a whisper. "Remember, Sorcha, everyone has their place."

THE TWILIGHT SKY PAINTS the world in shades of lavender and pink as Rian and I arrive at the glen Brian chose for our courtship date. The glen is beautiful, with its ethereal glow from the bioluminescent flowers and the gentle hum of magical creatures flitting about. It would have been the perfect setting for romance, had I had any mood for it.

"This is gorgeous!" Isabel says, hooking her arm in mine, the physical embodiment of the second reason my mood is sour tonight. The first reason is still attached to my wrist.

In that silent conversation between the two at the end of the council meeting, Rian and Isabel must have planned to jointly interrupt my courting date. Rian was already a required attendant, Isabel's participation simply adds to my bad luck. Perhaps she doesn't want to leave me alone with Rian any longer than she must, not if she's aware of our 'completion.' But regardless, their presence makes my already lousy chances at a good courtship—since I *will* be bound at Lughnasadh—even more dismal.

Brian doesn't seem terribly upset about our interlopers as he offers me a small smile, revealing gleaming white teeth. "It's good to meet you, Sorcha. I know you agreed this afternoon, but Fintan not receiving your attendance confirmation made me worry you might not actually appear." He takes my hand, his touch warm and firm, his palms calloused from years of writing with quills.

If I'd refused, Fintan and the elders would just come find me, and then I'd likely be paired up with someone repulsive. In the seconds Brian was presented to me earlier, he, at least, seemed unobjectionable. I shake his hand, Rian tight against my side. "Failing to confirm was because of a traveling issue," I try to explain. "I had a conflict that took me away from Avalaruin for a few days."

"I hope all is well," Brian says, brow furrowing.

My smile is strained. "As good as it can be," I confess, thinking of the chain hidden up my sleeve.

"Regardless, I am glad you're here." His gaze slides to Rian and Isabel. "Although I didn't realize this was a double date."

Rian slides an arm around my waist from the other side. "Ah, we're a package deal. Sorcha and

I... and Isabel. Can't go somewhere without the rest of us following."

I force a smile. "Right. That's right. We're the... terrific trio, after all."

Brian chuckles softly, his eyes twinkling with amusement. "Well, in that case, I'm glad to have the trio with us tonight."

Isabel squeals in excitement and pulls us both towards the heart of the glen where a small bonfire flickers to life, surrounded by soft pillows and blankets. Though I can feel no heat from it, the flames dance and cast a soft glow over our faces as we settle around it on plush cushions. My flames would be brighter, warmer too, and I quickly spark them to life. Better gain *some* comfort from this event.

Rian tries to help me settle on a fluffy cushion, but I bat his hands away. He sits beside me, leaning too close, with Isabel on my other side. Brian sits across from me, pulling out a small picnic basket. He ducks his chin, looking boyish, as he opens it.

"There's only enough for two," he explains, his eyes intent on my face. "I hadn't expected additional company. I hope that's alright."

"What's a little sharing between friends?" Rian says with a smile that's all teeth. "Shall we start with some wine?" he suggests, reaching for a bottle that sparkles with a faint inner light.

"That sounds wonderful," Isabel says, her smile still firmly in place. "Sorcha, you must try this. It's one of Rian's favorites."

I clench my teeth while accepting the glass Rian pours for me and decide to be blunt. "Brian, you and I are looking down the barrel of eternity here. What should I know about you before any binding?"

Rian shifts beside me, opening his mouth but I quickly elbow him. Again.

Brian's gaze softens as he looks at me again, his expression thoughtful. "Well, where to begin... I suppose the most important thing for you to know is that I value tradition. The decisions of our elders are to be honored and revered."

"But you've been bound four times?" Rian asks, his tone idle but his expression keen. "How many of those bindings were the elders' choices?"

Brian shoots Rian a pointed look. "All of them."

"Were the failures the blame of your partners or you?" Rian asks, propping his elbow on his knee and resting against his fist. The other, cuffed, hand is placed against my back, as if he's trying to soothe the hackles that will inevitably rise at this line of questioning.

Brian's jaw tenses for a moment before he takes a sip of his wine, his expression tight. "I believe it was a mutual issue."

"How lucky you received the freedom of another choice," Rian says, winking.

An uncomfortable silence settles over us, broken only by the crackling of the fire and the distant hum of insects. Isabel and Rian appear to be communicating again, this time with hand signals and eyebrow movements while Brian and I sit silently, likely both thinking about our failed bindings and the pressure on us. There's a spark of magic surrounding the tiresome twosome now; they've moved from miming to using illusions to block our hearing.

I open my mouth to say something, anything to Brian to stop the slow death of this date, but Isabel snaps her fingers and the illusion drops.

"Sorcha had four bindings as well," Isabel says. She leans forward, her eyes darting between the three of us. "Each one a failure but I'm *certain* this next will work out. After all, sometimes things can surprise you. You don't plan for it, but there is it, staring you in the face."

Rian takes the opportunity to subtly shift in his seat, blocking my view of Isabel and Brian with his body. Irritated, I pull on the back of his shirt until he returns to his previous position.

Isabel looks between us, before returning her attention to Brian. "Isn't that right, Brian?"

Brian's jaw clenches as he forces out a response through gritted teeth. "Yes, sometimes unexpected paths lead us to unexpected outcomes."

"No kidding," I mutter.

"But tradition is tradition," he adds. "And we must respect it, even *if* it leads to those unexpected outcomes."

"But you agree that choice is paramount," Rian says.

My brows furrow along with Brian's, but Isabel and Rian exchange a meaningful glance, indicating there's something more going on here that I'm not privy to.

"Choice in...?" he asks.

"In everything!" Rian exclaims, gesturing animatedly with his hands. He nearly reveals the cuff around our wrist, but my firm grip keeps it hidden behind me. "In some cases, the decisions made by our elders need to be... managed. For the sake of freedom of choice."

Brian inclines his head in agreement, a flicker of something unreadable crossing his features. "I suppose."

Rian claps his hands. "Wonderful, isn't that wonderful, dearest?" he says, leaning close to me.

"I think so," Isabel adds with a radiant smile.

"And I expect I'll have your vote as well," Rian says, reaching across the fire to pat Brian's shoulder.

"My vote for what?" Brian asks, now it's his and my turn to exchange a perplexed look.

"For my crown, of course," Rian says nonchalantly, as if he hasn't just dropped an exploding enchantment on our conversation.

My heart jumps into my throat. "What?"

"The council is pressing Rian to bind this season," Isabel explains, looking rather smug at the knowledge. "Thus, he will be taking his crown."

The beginning of a headache forms behind my eyes, but it quickly travels to my chest, the ache familiar.

"And I need two members of the illusion guild on my side, for whatever may come," Rian continues. He gives Isabel a charming smile. "I have one already, obviously. And Brian, you could be the second."

Brian looks as though he's been hit by a carriage. "I, ah, I'll stand behind the crown prince if asked," he says warily.

"Fantastic. That was easier than I thought. More wine?" Rian says breezily, acting as though he hasn't entirely upended the entire conversation.

Isabel breaks the confusing atmosphere with a bright smile. "Let's not dwell on the past tonight!

Let's think of the future and enjoy each other's company." She claps her hands together. "How about a game?"

Rian chuckles. "I love games! What did you have in mind, Isabel?"

She produces a deck of brightly colored cards out of thin air, a reminder of her magical abilities.

I grit my teeth in annoyance. "How about a game of riddles instead?"

Brian turns to me with relief in his eyes, likely grateful for the interruption from the dynamic duo's odd performance. "I enjoy a good riddle."

"Excellent!" I say determinedly. "I've got one about completion." I glance at Rian, whose jaw clenches tightly. "There are two people, magically bound, who must find the heart of their bond in order to complete it and break free from each other."

Brian furrows his brow. "That's an unusual riddle."

"That's what makes it fun," I reply dryly. "Any thoughts?"

Without warning, Rian snatches my wine glass and begins chugging the remaining contents. Isabel watches with gleaming eyes.

"Have they tried having sex?" Brian suggests casually.

Rian chokes on the wine, spilling it down his shirt. He exposes our chained wrist to clean himself, as Isabel leaps over his lap to dab away the liquid.

And, of course it only gets worse from there.

Chapter
12

With a resounding slam, I shut the door to my quaint cottage, the sound echoing through the empty hallway. Rian follows, the enchanted cuffs around our wrists jangling with every step. It takes three steps to cross to the far wall where my herbs and poultices hang. I snatch them up, my fingers turning into claws around the jars from frustration.

"What concoction are you whipping up now, dearest?" Rian asks, leaning against the wall and eyeing the ingredients with calm amusement. His tone may sound gentle, but there's a tension in his gaze that gives him away.

I let out a low growl and scowl up at him. "If I'm lucky, a poison."

He peers down at what I've gathered. "I may not be as skilled in charms as you—" Here he pauses to let me scowl up at him again. "But those ingredients won't create a poison."

My hands tighten around the jars as I slam them down onto the table. "Yes, but I'll try to make something that *isn't* a poison and it will, inevitably, create one."

Rian sighs, rubbing the back of his neck with his free hand. "I know this is stressful, love. I didn't expect Isabel to join the date either. She was simply—"

I jab a finger into his chest, hard. It likely hurts my finger more than his irritatingly toned body. "Neither of you should have been there. But, of course, she was there, always showing up for you." Heat curls through my stomach. Better to be mad than sad, Mama always said. "And now we're back here, still cuffed together, and I can't even enjoy what could be my last few months in my home without thinking about what's going to happen next."

"Darling—"

"No, Rian," I interrupt, my voice rising. "I'm tired of this. Tired of everything. The binding, the cuffs, the constant presence of Isabel. And now, I have to face the possibility of castigation or worse for magically cuffing myself to the crown prince!"

Brian's talk of tradition and 'revering' the decisions of the elders was double-speak that means he's run back to Desmond and Fintan already. None of them are wishcrafters, but certainly someone could cobble together an enchantment to melt the metal, whatever it takes to release their prince. They'll know I was reckless, that I didn't have the skill or strength to undo this mistake. They'll use it against me.

Rian reaches out, wrapping his hand around my finger, his other hand covering mine. "They won't dare lay a consequence on you. If I have to use every vote at my disposal, I'll make certain of it. In a few months time, no one will care a whit about this wish."

I ignore his insincere offer and instead glare up at him mutinously, yanking my hand out of his grasp. "Oh, I'm sure you will. And then I'll be known as the girl who needed the prince's votes to save her reputation. And I'll become a social pariah instead."

Rian's eyes soften, a hint of a wry smile tugging at his lips. "Are you not already one by choice?"

"Hilarious," I snap, crossing my arms over my chest and maintaining my defiant glare.

"Besides," he continues blithely, "Isabel's already informed the council." His expression remains calm as he watches my reaction, as if this revelation is nothing more than a minor inconvenience.

Blood drains from my face. After all my hard work, all my scheming to keep the damned cuffs out of sight, and Isobel...

"That wasn't up to her," I say, my voice dangerously low. "Or you."

Rian's face shifts, a flicker of discomfort quickly masked. "Sorcha, it isn't as bad as you think. The council understands—"

"Understands?" I interrupt, voice rising with each word. "They don't understand me, Rian! They'll see this as a mistake. They'll make me into an example, a warning for anyone else who thinks they might have a say in their own future."

I let out a bitter laugh, imagining the council's smug, judgmental faces, and anger heats me from the inside out. I can practically hear Fintan's condescending voice calling me a fool, Desmond's disappointed frown as he dismisses me as reckless and irresponsible. "They'll know I tried to take my name off the betrothal lists and see this as proof I can't be trusted to make my own decisions! You know that!"

Rian's mouth tightens, and he steps closer, grabbing my hand. "They will not punish you, I can promise you that."

"They don't see the bindings as punishment." I jerk my hand away. "You don't get it, Rian. You don't know what it's like."

"You believe I don't understand a life without choice?" His voice is low, and there's a flicker of frustration in his eyes.

"I believe you have privileges the rest of us don't," I bite back. "You haven't had to bind. Not once. You're the crown prince, Rian."

"The prince without a crown," he reminds me, his face unreadable.

"Until you choose a bride and the entire world is yours to command."

A charged silence follows, and Rian's expression shifts slightly, becoming something harder, unreadable. "You think that once I wear the crown, I'll suddenly have my freedom?"

"That's exactly what I think," I say, my tone measured. "You're the prince, Rian. You have options. You can choose to marry, or not, to change the rules if you wish. You could overthrow the whole damned council if you wanted, by simply batting your eyes until enough heirs to stand behind you. But I'm expected to make binding attempts, one after another, without question."

He shakes his head, a dark look settling into his eyes. "It isn't that simple, Sorcha. Do you think I don't want to change things? That I haven't tried? But there are layers to this, traditions I can't just shred without—"

"Without what?" I cut him off, frustration spilling over. "Without risking some of your power? Without angering the elders? At least you have the option to flex your power without consequence. Because that's what will happen to me. They'll make me an example, a cautionary tale for every other fae who dares to challenge them. And you..." My voice cracks, my emotion splintering. "You'll walk away unscathed."

This isn't what I wanted. None of this is what I wanted.

His eyes shutter, emotion slipping behind a mask I don't recognize. "Of course, darling. Forgive my... misunderstanding." He looks behind me and talks to the wall. "I might have another idea or two to remove the cuffs, if you'd grant me some privacy."

I raise an eyebrow, thrown by the detached edge to his voice. "Are you asking for privacy in *my* house? Considering, I don't know... we're shackled together?"

His gaze flicks down at me, his lips quirking, before the smile fades away again. "Like we did in the glen earlier. An illusion."

Understanding hits me like a bolt. Isabel. *Of course.* My face shutters then as I force the irritation away. "Right. That's fine. You can stand outside and I'll slip the chain through the opening in the door." I'd never fixed the draft, at least it can be useful now.

"Brilliant, dearest." The words sound sincere, but the tone is flat. "I'll go now."

Before I can say much more, we've maneuvered the chain through the biggest crack, one that nearly lets in snow during the winter, and I'm leaned against the door inside, just out of sight. Still, as irritated as I am, I can't resist a glance at the two of them. All the better to punish myself, I suppose. I press my cheek to the cool glass pane beside the door, catching a glimpse of them outside.

Rian runs a hand through his hair, his expression tight with frustration and something that almost looks like regret. Gone is his usual confidence, replaced by a restless energy, his eyes dark and stormy. Isabel stands opposite him, her face a careful mask of calm concern as she places a hand on his arm, the gesture tender and infuriatingly familiar. He shakes his head, motioning toward the ground, then the closed door, his lips moving too fast for me to decipher his words. Isabel's brows draw together as she listens, nodding slowly.

My stomach churns with suspicion. *Is he telling her... about us having sex?* For someone who's supposed to be his future wife, Isabel doesn't seem remotely upset. If anything, she seems to soften, her hand lingering on his shoulder, as if she's comforting him through a difficult confession.

Isabel's eyes flick toward the glass, making me leap back, pressing myself against the door. When I peek again, Rian has turned away from Isabel, rubbing his face with both hands. Isabel steps closer to him, refusing to let him turn from her, placing both hands on his shoulders. My imagination runs wild, filling in the gaps of their silent conversation. Was Isabel accepting his apology for sleeping with me? Was she suggesting ways to make things right? Was she telling him to throw me to the wolves?

Rian nods slowly, his posture relaxing as Isabel continues to speak. Her hand moves from Rian's shoulder to his cheek, a soft and comforting gesture. My chest tightens as I turn to slide down the wall, resting on the floor with my arms around my knees, chain trailing outside. It hadn't occurred to me just how upset Rian must be about this situation. He always played the role of the rake, has done ever since we were in our twenties. But now, as I watch him through the glass, I can see the turmoil and conflict clearly etched on his face.

Have I misread everything? What else might I have missed?

I WAS TWENTY-THREE YEARS old.

I stood in the center of the ceremonial chamber, surrounded by ancient stone walls that seemed to hold centuries worth of secrets. The flickering candlelight danced across the rough surfaces, casting long, prancing shadows that mocked the solemnity of my current situation. Noel stood opposite me, his once handsome face now a mask of resignation and disappointment. Our binding had just been undone, after a year and a day of marriage that had never truly bloomed into something real. The golden thread that had symbolized our bond now lay on the floor, dull and lifeless. Like our relationship.

I sighed, feeling a mix of relief and sadness. I looked at Noel, who, no matter how I'd refused to admit it during our marriage, bore an uncanny resemblance to Rian—same piercing eyes, same strong jawline, and even similar mannerisms. Looking back on it, it was clearly part of why I'd agreed to bind with him, hoping that maybe I could find some semblance of happiness with someone so much like the man I loved. But it hadn't worked out that way. I could only hope that the council chose someone very different for my next round.

"I suppose that's that," I said, trying to keep my tone light as I turned to leave the chamber. "I'm sure I'll see you around, Noel. Good luck with your next binding."

But before I could take another step, Noel's voice stopped me.

"Sorcha, wait."

I paused, turning back to face him. "What is it?"

He took a deep breath, as if gathering his thoughts before speaking. "We're both heading into another binding season, but…"

My eyebrows raised in curiosity as I waited for him to continue.

"You never give enough of yourself, Sorcha," he said, sounding frustrated. "You're always holding back. Even when we were bound, it felt like you had one foot out the door, always waiting for something—or someone—else."

My defenses rose at his accusation. "That's not fair, Noel. I tried. I really did."

Noel shook his head, a bitter smile playing on his lips. "Maybe you did. But it was never enough." He softens his tone. "I'm not angry, Sorcha. Just... disappointed. I thought maybe we could find something real between us. But you were always somewhere else, not in life but in your thoughts, with someone else."

I shrugged, unwilling to explain myself to him now that our binding had been broken. I owed him nothing.

Noel sighed, running a hand through his long black hair. "I'm sorry. I simply thought it might be something to consider before we both head into another binding season. But until you let go of whatever is holding you back, you'll never truly be free."

I nodded, trying to swallow the lump in my throat. "Right. Well. Thanks, I guess." I turned to leave once again.

Noel called after me, "I hope you find what you're looking for, Sorcha. You deserve that. We both do."

Chapter 13

DAWN CREEPS THROUGH THE gauzy curtains of my bedroom. I'd been awake for hours, lost in thought as I sat at the edge of my childhood bed.

Beside me, Rian lays still, his breaths deep and steady, the chaos of the previous night now replaced with a tranquil calm. My childhood bed felt even smaller with both of us in it, but I couldn't bring myself to suggest anything more comfortable after seeing his frustration and pain last night.

As he starts to stretch and reach out for me, I stiffen and clear my throat to wake him. "Good morning," I say hesitantly.

"Good morning," he replies, his voice low. But despite the warmth in his eyes, tension still hangs between us.

"I'm sorry for upsetting you yesterday," I say softly, avoiding his gaze and instead focusing on the rumpled sheets. "You didn't ask for any of this either."

Rian reaches over, his fingers tracing a gentle line along my jaw and I hold my breath, unsure if I want to surrender to the touch or recoil away. "You did nothing wrong," he murmurs reassuringly. "And I should have seen it from your perspective. I should not have told the council without speaking with you first."

I meet his gaze, a bit of the tightness loosening from my chest. The apology softens something inside me, but the memory of his words and the frustration from last night still lingers, faint but present. I take a slow breath, letting the weight of everything settle between us, to feel the old familiar comfort of his presence.

But our entwined fates cannot be ignored. With a reluctant sigh, I push against his chest, the movement more plea than force. "We need to go back to the library—or maybe leave Avalaruin again. Perhaps the human mages will have some idea. Anything to discover how to 'complete' the bond."

Rian's hand closes gently around mine, halting its retreat. "We can search again tomorrow," he says with a hint of playfulness in his tone. "But today, we have other plans."

Confusion furrows my brow. "Other plans? I wasn't aware of any plans…"

A secretive smile tugs at the corners of his lips. "I've arranged a surprise ball," he admits with a mischievous glint in his eyes. "We all could use some fun, don't you think? And it's also the perfect opportunity for me to announce my intention to take my crown this year. Plus," he adds with a wink, "we might as well get ahead of the rumors about us being 'handcuffed' together."

The idea of a ball—a celebration amidst all our uncertainty, putting my mistake on display—feels foreign and strange.

"Surprise indeed," I manage to say, the mix of emotions within me swirling like the hem of a gown in a waltz. "Is this what you and Isabel planned yesterday?"

His smile fades, but only just. "Always thinking of Isabel."

Because it's always her. My shrug is stilted, because of our position on the bed and nothing else. "It was just a question."

He sighs, shaking his head slightly, his dark hair falling over his eyes. Inhaling deeply, I reach out and use my fingers to gently brush his hair back and away from his face. He captures my hand and presses a kiss to my palm.

"We'll have fun tonight, dearest," he says with a twinkle in his eye. "I've planned the best for my... accomplice in cuffs." His grin is roguish, his eyes alight with mischief. But even as he leans in again to brush his lips against my forehead, my mind races ahead, contemplating the price of this ball.

THE GRANDEUR OF THE ballroom unfolds before me like a scene plucked from my imagination. The ball that announced Rian as eligible for the binding pales compared to what he's created for tonight, like a faded watercolor to this vibrant and opulent oil painting. Towering columns wrapped in winding roses soar above to newly frescoed ceilings, where painted gods and goddesses gaze down upon the revelry with silent approval. Crystal chandeliers drip from above, spilling soft golden firelight over the assembly below. Every corner of the room is filled with splendor, from the colossal flower arrangements to the glittering outfits of the guests. How he pulled this together in less than a day speaks to the magical skill of our community and his power when he'll take the mantle of High King.

My heels click against the polished marble floor, echoing the rhythmic heartbeat of the orchestra. Violins sing a sweet lament that swirls around us, entwining with the deeper notes of cellos in an enchanting dance. The air itself seems to shimmer, scented with the blend of a hundred perfumes and colognes. One of Rian's servants dropped off our outfits; tonight we're clad in silver—the color of the cuffs—with Rian wearing a small antlered crown atop his wild hair.

But amidst all the splendor and elegance, a coil of unease tightens within me. I can feel the weight of every glance that slides my way, the whisper of silk against metal a souvenir of my predicament, the sensation of Rian's arm hooked around mine a reminder of why I shouldn't be here. Isabel's icy gaze cuts through the throng, her elegant facade not concealing her disdain as she sneers in our direction. She's the only one with outright contempt on her expression, but I expect the rest to follow soon. With a practiced smile, I lift my chin, though my hands seek refuge in the folds of my gown, subtly concealing the cuffs. It's a futile gesture as the cool metal seems to pulse against my skin.

"Are you well?" Rian murmurs, his hand finding the small of my back, guiding me forward. His touch is possibly meant to reassure, or rile me as he likes to do, but it only serves to heighten my awareness of the attention on us.

"Everyone's staring," I whisper back, though my words are lost amidst the music and laughter.

"Let them stare," he says with a gentle defiance that was so characteristic of him, "They'll see nothing but our beauty."

But I'm not so certain. I can sense their curiosity and judgment. It's hard to enjoy myself under the weight of the room's stares and whispers.

"Sorcha, let us forget the cuffs for a moment and simply enjoy ourselves," Rian coaxes, his voice soft against the melody. "I have an announcement to come that I believe you'll enjoy."

Just then, Isabel catches his attention. They share a look, another one of those silent conversations that seems to carry more weight than words. Turning back to me, he offers a stilted smile surrounded by an unreadable expression. "After I speak with Isabel, that is."

He leads me to a secluded alcove. The cuffs around my wrists feel heavier with each step. I awkwardly stand outside it, arm outstretched, as he and Isabel enter. His hand touches her arm, and the air around them shimmers subtly—a sure sign of another of Isabel's illusions at work. The sounds of their private world are muffled, leaving only the ghost of whispers to reach my straining ears. She's draped in emerald silk that catches the light like the sheen of leaves after rain. Together they paint a picture of opulence and beauty.

Curiosity, burning brighter than the chandeliers above, draws me closer. I Inch forward, the gossamer fabric of my gown whispering against the polished floor as I strain to catch the fragments of their whispers, but her illusion holds. One foot steps over the threshold, breaking the enclosure of Isabel's magic. The illusion flickers for a moment, and suddenly I can hear their conversation.

"What do you *mean* it isn't working?" Her words, though faint, strike through the music and festivity, landing with a weighty silence in my chest.

I freeze, my heart pounding as the world around me fades into a blur of colors and shadows.

Rian's response is barely a murmur, but it feels like a slap to my senses. "It's not time yet. We need to wait for the right moment."

My mind races, trying to make sense of their cryptic conversation. What isn't working? What right moment are they waiting for?

"Rian," Isabel's voice is tinged with a caution that sends icy fingers of dread racing up my spine,

"Your intentions are noble, but let us not forget the spectacle it would create."

The word 'spectacle' echoes within me, mocking the opulent surroundings of the ballroom. Here, amidst the splendor of twinkling chandeliers and nobles twirling in an endless dance, *I* am a spectacle. A misfit cuffed to the prince, the man on the cusp of taking his crown and binding to his queen, Isabel.

"Sorcha has a role to play, certainly," Rian replies sharply, his words slicing through the air like a blade unsheathed. "And after tonight, no one will question the strength of our alliance—or its necessity."

Alliance? Necessity? The terms they used are cold, a far cry from the tenderness, the *friendship*, he'd been showing me. A shroud of confusion envelopes me, as my heart, a frenzied drumbeat against my ribs, seems intent on betraying my presence with its thunderous echo.

"Alright. You may have *your* wish, my King," Isabel murmurs, her laughter a silken thread in a dark tapestry. "By morning, the entire kingdom will be abuzz with the news. And Sorcha... I suppose she will be none the wiser about all these machinations."

The murmur of the crowd becomes a roar in my ears, each laugh and snippet of conversation a wave crashing over me as anger and humiliation heat my cheeks. My vision blurs, a cascade of tears threatening to break free as the realization dawns upon me like the first light of dawn—harsh, unyielding, inevitable.

This was all a ploy to embarrass me. For what? I can't guess. It isn't as though the powerful need a reason to tease the lesser. My childhood memories show the truth of that.

"Rian, do not forget who you are," Isabel says, leaning in and cupping his cheeks in her hands. "Do what must be done and let the pieces fall where they may."

The world tilts. Betrayal wraps its icy fingers around my heart, squeezing until the pain is all-consuming, unbearable. I realize what I'd given him. What I gave him years earlier and hoped I'd taken back, but every minute cuffed to him proved I hadn't. It wasn't power; it was my heart.

And it just unceremoniously shattered.

A sharp sensation snaps against my skin—the cuffs. I gasp, the sound lost amidst the swell of music and laughter that fills the room. Heat suffuses my wrist until a faint crack materializes along the delicate filigree, a spiderweb of fracture lines spreading across the surface, bubbling as though the metal is dissolving from within. As if responding to my shattered spirit, the cuffs melt and burst with a sound akin to a whispered secret, a faint echo of release.

The remnants of our bond lie scattered on the polished marble floor, catching the light from the chandeliers above like a constellation of fallen stars. My gaze settles on the broken cuffs, a blend of relief and devastation surging through me with the intensity of a tempest. Relieved that I'm no longer shackled to a lie, yet devastated by the gaping void where my... love once was.

"Sorcha..." The word, wrought with alarm, pierces through the haze of my pain.

I turn slowly, as if awakening from a dream—or perhaps falling deeper into a nightmare. Rian is there, his features contorted with shock. His eyes, those pools of ice-blue, now mirror my own disbelief.

"Wh-what happened?" His voice trembles. He reaches out, but I recoil instinctively.

"Look," I whisper, my voice barely audible over the music that continues its haunting melody, oblivious to the drama unfolding in its midst. "Your surprise ball... and now this." A bitter laugh escapes me, tinged with the sorrow of a heart too tired to maintain its composure.

"Sorcha, please," Rian implores. He takes an uncertain step closer, his hand outstretched as though he could mend the shattered pieces with his touch alone. "This can't be what it seems. You must believe me—"

"Believe you?" The question hangs between us. "When all I've heard are sweet words laced with deceit?"

"Deceit?" His brow furrows, and for a minute, he seems genuinely perplexed. "No, you misunderstand. It's not—"

"Enough, Rian." My voice cuts through the air, sharper than any blade. "It doesn't matter. The cuffs are broken. I'm going home."

His hand falls to his side, and something within him falters—a glimpse of vulnerability that he rarely shows, something I hadn't seen so fiercely since we were sixteen.

"I planned this ball for us," he whispers, like he's talking to himself rather than to me. "To bring joy amidst the chaos, to celebrate..."

"Celebrate?" I echo, incredulity seeping into my tone. "Celebrate this 'alliance' you have made with Isabel while I play my role as... what? The hapless childhood friend to further shore up support for your crown? Look at our High King, how kind he is even to the lesser of us."

"No, of course not," Rian nearly growls. "Let me explain." He reaches out again, his hand brushing against mine.

But I pull back slowly, my voice hollow and distant. "No." Tears well in my eyes and scrape them away with my two free hands. My wrists feel light—a stark contrast against the heaviness in my chest.

"Sorcha, there is nothing I wouldn't do to prove my sincerity to you. This was all for you." His voice is thick with emotion, each word dripping with urgency. "Let me show you. Please. The announcement," he's nearly panting now, "it will explain everything."

But explanations will not mend a broken heart, or restore a trust that has been fractured. The voice sounds like Mama's.

My eyes continue to sting, but I will not cry in front of him. "You may have orchestrated a grand spectacle, Rian, but tonight, the greatest performance is the one you played on me. And I will not allow it to happen again."

Rian reaches for me again, his voice a desperate whisper against the chaos of the ballroom. It's a wonder our own spectacle isn't taking center stage. "Don't do this," he pleads.

I recoil from his touch as though it's a flame, my gaze darting between him and Isabel who stands behind him. *She'd tried to warn me yesterday*, I realize. With all her talk of 'roles.'

It's because of that... *modicum* of politeness she gave me, and my own self-preservation, that I'll let this go. Rather than confront them or unleash the tempest of questions and accusations swirling within me. Instead, I'll dissolve into the shadows and escape the weight of countless eyes will likely bear into me, seeking out the scandal they hunger for.

"Rian," I manage, my voice barely my own. "You've received your performance. Now let me leave with what little dignity I have left."

"Sorcha, you don't understand—"

But understanding is a luxury I can't give, not when every fiber of my being screams in betrayal. The urge to vanish from this opulent prison grows overpowering; the need for air, for space, for freedom consumes me. With faltering steps, I turn away from him, from the whispers, from the coming scrutiny of the court, and from the piercing gaze of the man I can no longer allow myself to trust.

"Heartbreak is the price of freedom," I whisper to myself, trying to find strength in those words.

I reach the grand doors of the ballroom, the cool night air brushing against my skin like the softest of caresses, promising solace and solitude beyond. With each step toward the threshold, the cacophony dims, and the tumult within me wanes, replaced by a fragile peace laced with the sharp tang of loss.

Just before crossing the boundary between the world I know and the unknown that beckons, I pause, my hand trembling on the door's ornate handle. Tossing a final glance over my shoulder, I see him standing there, a figure etched in light and regret, reaching out to a ghost already gone. Behind me is a past fraught with misunderstanding and manipulation; ahead, a future uncertain but unfettered. In that suspended moment, the choice is mine alone.

And so, with the shards of a bond that had both constricted and defined me lying forgotten on the ballroom floor, I step into the night, feeling like I've lit an inferno.

Chapter
14

A MONTH TIPTOES BY, bringing with it a hushed and solitary stillness. I spend my days flitting about my cottage, packing and unpacking my belongings in a never-ending cycle. I've done it half a dozen times since my heart broke.

Oh certainly, letters come. They all sit in a haphazard pile outside my door: demands for courtship dates, invitations, apologies, pleas. On the day after that disastrous party, letters came every hour. Rian did too, but he never breached my door, staying outside, begging my forgiveness through the door. So as not to be forced to listen to him, I retreated to my childhood bedroom, but the walls were so thin I still heard him. I'm sure he heard tears fall as my emotions consumed me once I was finally alone. That night was the first time I packed my bags, only to unpack them again the next morning. And again and again.

The only correspondence I opened was from Phaeron. I'd sparked a conversation between us, sending over a few faelights sealed in glass jars and he'd responded with generous payments. My heightened emotions let the flames come much easier now. Even with my faulty magic, at least I can support myself. Whatever I may do.

Wind whispers from the open window, carrying the scent of rain and wildflowers from the surrounding forest. The moon hangs high, a silver sickle against the velvet night, casting a pale light that seems to question my every thought. I feel as though I'm trapped in a cage of my own making—one of indecision.

"Choices, choice," I mutter, each a chain, a shackle. Even though I'm free of the cuffs and the burden of loving Rian, my problems remain.

I could leave tonight, slip away in the dark like a wisp of mist in the forest. Vanish to the Aboveground, to the Vampire District or beyond, with unknown creatures and unfamiliar lands. Or I could stay in Avalaruin and join with the Fomorians, become a dark thing that dwells in the forest's depths. Let myself be consumed by the fire. Start anew, in a new form.

I could remain and bind myself to another fae, forever tethering my soul to a stranger.

My thoughts drift to Mama, as they often do when I'm in this cottage. I wonder how she managed it. She never bound, but she had me. I wasn't a surprise, she always said, but a gift. Was it my presence that kept her free from the elder's binding shackles? I huff at the thought. My only hope for a child would be the recent encounter with Rian, and that wouldn't free me from binding but make things so much worse.

A rustling from the underbrush snags my attention, and another letter now perches atop the growing pile. Not just any letter, but one sealed with wax the color of blood, stamped with the sigil of the elder council. This... this is different.

I slip outside to break the seal and unfold the parchment, the paper crackling softly in the quiet of my night. The words inscribed upon it are precise, formal, commanding my presence at the Council House at dawn. An elder summons—a rare honor or a foreboding omen, I can't decipher. Yes, I've ignored at least two courtship date requests, but Lughnasadh remains a month away. There is no reason for them to see me.

Unless I'm to be punished for the handcuffs, and my leaving Rian that night means they're all seeking retribution.

I shake the thought away. Being free of him must mean being free of fear. I did nothing wrong. With a deep breath that fills my lungs with the night's chill, I resolve to go.

Whatever lies ahead, I have to face it without hesitation or regret.

I SLIP THROUGH THE heavy oaken doors to the Council House like a shadow, my presence unnoticed by the guards whose eyes seek more conspicuous threats. My heart hammers against my ribs as I scan the room for familiar faces.

Inside, the air is thick with whispers and the scent of beeswax from the candles that line the wall. Heirs sit scattered around, their expressions tense as they wait for the proceedings to begin. From my vantage point, I see Brian writing frantically, his brow creased. Brennan, Marcus, all the others are present. The elders sit perched along their tall platform at the front of the room, their usual somber expressions present. But today is different. For the first time since the High King's death, someone sits at the head of the chamber above them, still wearing his antlered crown. I take a deep breath, willing myself to blend into the wooden bench beneath me and remain unseen.

Rian rises, his voice echoing throughout the expanse. "It is settled. The aquatic shapeshifter forum will be a week hence. Now, bring forth the accused," he commands, his words laced with an authority that demands obedience. Power oozes from him, stronger than usual. Even the elders seem to defer to him more than they have in the past.

But my thoughts on Rian shutter as Jackson emerges from the throng. He seems small compared to the empty grandeur of the surroundings, but he remains swollen with defiance. He meets Rian's gaze, unflinching, though the room seems to contract around him.

"Jackson of the Fae," Rian says, his tone even but cut with something dark, violent. "You stand before this council accused of abuse, a violation most vile against those entrusted to you."

My pulse quickens, each beat a crack in the facade of my composure. Is this why I was brought here? The thought of being named, of being forced to reveal my experiences with Jackson, fills me with dread.

As Jackson stammers through his defense, a string of excuses and denials, Rian's gaze sweeps over the room—a predator's search for prey hidden amidst a forest. I will myself to become part of the wooden bench, indistinguishable from the architecture of the court.

A spike of heat traces the length of my spine as the air in the chamber shifts, the faint whisper of magic threading through the charged silence. Beside me, like a shadow given form, Isabel materializes with a sly grin on her pouty red lips.

"An illusion," she murmurs. "For delicate matters like this, to keep prying eyes blind to the council's workings. I let you into it." With a graceful sweep of her hand, the room wavers and blurs around us, likely obscuring our visibility further until we are invisible to all but each other. "No one can see you but you can see them."

"Handy trick," I can't help but remark, my voice edged with sarcasm. "Are you also a mind reader?"

Isabel laughs softly, her voice dancing around us like a light breeze. "No need for such abilities when your presence is as loud as your silence, Sorcha."

"Enough!" Rian's sharp command cuts through our private whispers, his voice a blade.

"The evidence speaks with a clarity you lack, Jackson. This council will deliberate your fate, but know this: justice shall be served."

A heavy silence settles over the chamber as Rian and the elders discuss without our hearing. His expression darkens with each passing moment, his antlered crown seeming to glow with an ethereal light. The debate appears to ebb and flow like a tumultuous river, their expressions rising and falling like waves crashing against jagged rocks. Until finally, Rian slices his hand through the air and the illusion of silence drops. With it, whatever force was holding back Rian's rage also falls away, replaced by a new sense of power that borders on fury.

"Prison," Rian declares, his voice echoing off the ancient stones, "will be your punishment."

Jackson's chains clink a mournful dirge as the guards secure him, and he spits venomous words at Rian and the elders, his face twisted in fury. But Rian won't have it.

Shadows stretch long and menacing across the floor, crawling up the walls like dark, malevolent tendrils. Rian's silhouette grows, towering over the room, his antlered crown transforming into jagged claws, his features contorting into something primal, something monstrous and dangerous.

"Be grateful," he snarls at Jackson, each word a growl of barely contained rage, "that the elders temper my anger. For if it were solely my decision, Jackson, death would be a mercy I'd deny you for your crimes."

My heart thunders, a wild thing in my chest, as I watch the man I had once loved embody the ferocity of an untamed forest.

The room falls into an eerie stillness as Jackson is dragged away. Rian shifts back into his usual guise, but my gaze lingers on him, his monstrous silhouette a stark contrast to his typical appearance. Was this why he had summoned me here? To witness Jackson's downfall and see the true extent of Rian's power?

"Is this why?" I ask Isabel quietly. "Did Rian bring me here to see this?"

Isabel shakes her head. "No, Sorcha. This was justice. He doesn't know you're here. None of them do."

"Then why am I here?" There's a sharp edge to my question, honed by irritation and the shards of a heart not yet mended.

"Because you need to see what comes next." Isabel's eyes were pools of mystery, reflecting a purpose I can't fathom.

Rian rises, leaving his throne on the platform and stalking to the floor. Lights—both fire and faelight—brighten and the chamber is revealed. The few heirs I'd seen scattered throughout the room multiple into dozens, unveiling every heir, every fae not yet bound, even some that are. The room is packed.

Rian sweeps his gaze over the assembly, a sea of faces cloaked in expectation. Then he turns back to the elders, the antlered crown casting elongated shadows across his brow.

"Esteemed members," he begins, voice resonating with a power that seems to ripple through the very air, "I bring forth a resolution to abolish the archaic practice of mandatory bindings among our kind."

A murmur ripples through the crowd, shock (or expectation?) crashing against the high stone walls. My gasp echoes it. The elders, perched like ancient ravens on their high seats, exchange glances laced with disapproval.

"Bindings should be a choice, born of love or alliance, not a mandate from those who wield power without understanding its price," Rian continues, his words a blade slicing through centuries of tradition.

"High King Rian," Fintan retorts, his voice steeped in the weight of years, "you propose to unravel the very fabric that holds our society together. Bindings ensure stability and lineage."

Another gasp escapes my lips. *High King?*

"Stability?" A low growl rumbles from Rian's throat, his eyes flashing with an ire that turns the air thick. "What stability is there in forced unions? What lineage is preserved when hearts are shackled in resentment?"

"Bold words for one who has yet to secure his own binding," sneers Morrigan, her lips curling like the edges of a wilted leaf. "Was it not a month prior you came before this room and announced your intent to bind at Lughnasadh?"

"Ah," Rian says, the corner of his mouth twitching in a semblance of a smirk. "But it is there where you mistake my intention. My authority does not hinge on whom I bind myself to. You know this. My power stands upon the will of the people." He locks eyes with each elder, a silent challenge burning in his gaze. And as if by some unspoken cue, every person in the room rises to stand with him.

My breath catches and I snag Isabel's sleeve, ironic that she is my anchor when she's also been my long feared storm. "Does this mean?"

"Rian has taken the mantle of High King without a bride," she murmurs, her gaze not on the proceedings but on me, her eyes sharp as flint.

The revelation hits me like the shockwave from a fallen star. I jolt, my gaze snapping to the tip of Isabel's head, a place where a queen's circlet would rest—if there were a queen. Her wild curls are tamed by delicate floral clips instead of the regal crown she was always destined to wear.

"Without a... But how? He would need—" My words tangle in confusion, frayed at the edges by the implications.

"Power comes in many forms, Sorcha," Isabel replies, her lips twisting into a wry smile. "And he has seized it without binding himself to another. It's unprecedented."

"Unprecedented," I echo hollowly, the word foreign and strange on my tongue. The room spins, a vortex of faces and voices, but none so compelling as the figure of the high king.

"He's been planning it for months," Isabel adds.

"And what of the votes, High King?" challenges Desmond, his skepticism a tangible force.

"Secured," Rian snarls, antlers seeming to bristle with his determination. "And should any of you question my resolve, know this—I am now the High King with the authority to remove you all. Consider your positions precarious at best. This council will no longer dictate personal fates."

My breath catches as I watch him, a tempest cloaked in flesh. The elders recoil, their whispers like the hiss of wind through autumn leaves. Rian stands defiant, a lone sentinel against the tide of tradition, wielding his newfound power like a beacon.

"Are you not pleased?" Isabel's voice cuts through the chaos, smooth as river stones. She glances at me, her expression inscrutable.

"By what?" I scoff, masking my confusion and shock with a barbed quip. "I assumed the antlered crown was your goal, Isabel. Yet here you stand, sans diadem. A pity—horns would've suited you."

She laughs, clear and bright. "Oh, Sorcha, always so quick to presume. I never wanted a crown, let alone a king."

"But you were destined for each other." The words tumble from my lips, jagged and raw, still laced with the shock that clings to me like the morning dew on a spider's silk. It's unfathomable, this twist in the tale I had woven in my mind.

Isabel's smile holds a bittersweet wisdom. "Both of you are so short-sighted. Never looking at what's directly in front of you."

I frown. "Explain," I ask, barely above a whisper amidst the tempest that swirls around us.

"Those cuffs," Isabel begins, gesturing towards where the shimmering golden cuff once encircled my wrist. "They were all Rian's idea."

"His idea?" I'd be crowing in triumph if my heart weren't already in my stomach from the weight of these revelations.

"Indeed," Isabel confirms. "You had been ignoring him since your twentieth summer. When he overheard your half-formed wish… he saw it as his best chance, his last chance."

"Last chance?" My heart twists painfully at her words, caught in a whirlwind of conflicting emotions and sudden clarity.

"Before you were bound again. I advised him to simply tell you his heart, stop playing the games." Isabel's voice softens. "But Rian, he always felt bound by duty, by the role he must play. If you were seen together, it would soften the surprise of your union, introduce the elders to your alliance."

My breath hitches, trapped within the confines of my chest as if held by an unseen force. "The emergent council meeting," I realize.

"He wanted to convince you to choose him, to bind yourself to him, truly and forever," she continues, her eyes holding mine with an intensity that left no room for doubt. "Every minute those cuffs remained, it meant he still had hope. It meant you hadn't rejected him outright, that perhaps you still harbored a desire to bind with him."

"He was never yours?" My question hangs between us.

"Never," she confirms without hesitation. "He has always belonged to you. No one else could dare to try."

Each minute, each silent plea encapsulated in the cold metal that had graced my skin. I *knew* I hadn't wished it that way. And through it all, Rian had been waiting, watching, hoping.

Around us, the chamber thrums with the undercurrent of change. My gaze is drawn again to Rian, who stands resolute amidst the sea of contention—a beacon of change in a world reluctant to relinquish its grasp on the old ways. And yet, the ache in my heart whispers of lost chances and unspoken truths.

But hope, like I'd learned eight years ago, lingers, ready to sprout even in barren fields. "Always mine," I say, the words tasting of possibility, of paths not yet taken.

But does this repair the trust that was broken? Does it heal a shattered heart?

"Now, Sorcha." Isabel's voice pulls me back from my introspection. "What will you do with this knowledge? And the freedom *not* to bind, only if you wish it."

The question lingers, heavy with the weight of choices I never knew I had. As I contemplate the consequences of Rian's actions, the gravity of those choices yet to be made settles upon my shoulders.

"I don't know," I admit.

Chapter 15

I was fourteen years old.

I still had one more year with Mama, she didn't get sick until a few months after this rosy afternoon.

The clearing behind our cottage was alive with the scent of herbs and the distant hum of the forest. I sat cross-legged on a blanket, the same one I used for my misbegotten ritual. Mama knelt beside me, weaving together a garland of lavender and sage with deft fingers.

"You seem quiet today," she remarked gently, her sharp eyes catching every twitch of my restless hands.

"I'm just thinking," I muttered, plucking at the edge of the blanket.

"Thinking about what?"

I hesitated, my fingers stilling as a lump formed in my throat. I stared at the garland Mama was working on, its small, perfect blossoms lined up with care. "About how everyone else seems to know what they want. Where they belong. I don't know. I don't even know if I *can* know."

Mama paused, setting the garland aside. "Why are you thinking about this now, love? What's made you feel this way?"

My eyes darted away, toward the line of trees that separated our small home and field from the rest of Avalaruin. "There was a gathering of the heirs last night," I began haltingly. "Rian invited me. All the others were there, everyone else our age. They were talking about what they want to do after they come of age. Where they want to be. Who they want to bind to someday."

Mama tilted her head, waiting patiently.

"They all sounded so... sure," I admitted, my voice cracking. "Isabel will join the illusion guild and take over her mother's landlording. Rian—he said he'd make his father proud and take the crown the minute he can." Which meant marrying someone, but I didn't tell Mama my thoughts on that.

Instead, I gave a bitter laugh. "Even Roland said he was going to open a bakery, of all things."

"And what about you?" Mama asked gently.

"I said nothing," I confessed, my voice small. "What could I say? I can't cast a charm without it going sideways. I figured I'd take over the apothecary, with you, but none of my tinctures ever turn out. I don't know what I want, Mama. I don't even know if I belong here."

Mama's gaze softened, and she reached out, tucking a stray curl behind my ear. "You're feeling this way because you think you have to have all the answers right now," she said. "But, love, you don't."

I shook my head, frustration bubbling up. "But everyone else does! They have their magic, their plans, their place. And me? I'm just... here."

Mama's hands found mine, squeezing them gently. "Listen to me, Sorcha. You're not just 'here.' You're growing, learning, finding your way. And that takes time."

"But what if I never find it?" I whispered, looking down at the lines of her fingers, the scratches from knife cuts and wrinkles from scouring the cauldrons. "What if there's no place for me?"

Mama smiled faintly, her expression a mix of tenderness and steel. "Belonging isn't about fitting into a place that's already there. It's about carving out a space for yourself. Choosing where you want to be, and who you want to be with. And if that space doesn't exist yet, you make it."

I swallowed hard, my chest tight. "But how? How do I even start?"

Mama tilted her head toward the horizon, where the light of the sun was fading into the shadows of the forest. "You start by listening to yourself. What makes you feel alive? What do you want—not what others expect of you, but what you *truly* want?"

"I don't know," I murmured.

"Then that's your first choice: to start figuring it out. And it's okay if it takes time. What matters is that you keep choosing. Don't let fear or doubt choose for you. Don't let other people's paths distract you from finding your own." Mama squeezed my hands again. "And never forget: your life, your choices, are yours alone to make. No one can take that from you—not the elders, not tradition, not even your own doubts."

We sat in silence for a moment, the forest alive with the hum of crickets and the soft rustling of leaves.

I thought of Rian, of the easy confidence in his voice when he'd spoken of his future. How he'd smiled at Isabel when she laughed about joining the illusion guild, as though the world already made sense to them both.

"I just feel so far behind," I admitted finally.

Mama's gaze grew sharp. "There's no race, love. The only measure that matters is your own. And you'll get there—not by following others, but by listening to your own heart. You don't have to know everything right now, Sorcha."

I frowned. "But what if I make the wrong choice? What if—what if I ruin everything?"

Mama's laughter was soft but warm, like sunlight filtering through leaves. "Oh, love. There's no such thing as a perfect choice. Every path you take will come with challenges and sacrifices. But the only 'wrong' choice is the one made for you, not by you."

The Council House empties, the soft murmurs and shuffling footsteps fading until silence fills the chamber. I remain seated in the back row, cloaked in the safety of Isabel's illusion, watching the last council member drift out the door. Shadows stretch and dance across the vast room, draping over empty benches and lingering in the dim corners.

The chamber feels more expansive now, almost cavernous, with everyone gone. The weight of what lies ahead presses down on me, but for once, I don't want to escape it. It's a rare moment of solitude, a gift, and the time I need to finally face what I've been avoiding for too long.

"No one would blame me for walking away," I tell the empty air. Not now that I have the choice.

I want to be free. Free from the expectations, the bindings, the obligations that others have tried to force upon me. My entire life has been a struggle for control, for autonomy, for the right to make my own choices. And I have it, finally.

Then what am I still afraid of?

My uncertainty lingers in the air like a menacing storm cloud. I close my eyes and breathe deeply, letting the memories rise, each one sharper and more vibrant than the last. The looks Rian has given me, the way his laughter brightens the dullest day, the warmth of his touch even when I felt frozen inside. *He's always been mine*, Isabel said.

Can I finally be his?

The thought lingers in my mind, a seed of doubt that threatens to choke the fragile bloom of hope unfurling within me. To choose him—without fear, without hesitation—means embracing a future I can't fully control. It means taking a leap into the unknown, accepting the risk, and allowing myself to be vulnerable in ways I've never allowed before. In ways I've imagined but refused to let occur.

I draw a shuddering breath, my mind clearing as if I'm standing at the edge of something vast and beautiful. A warmth spreads through me, gentle yet insistent, like a light breaking through the dark. It's terrifying, exhilarating. And it's mine.

He's mine.

Slowly, I stand, the weight of my fear lifting with each breath. My feet feel lighter as I move toward the door, my pulse racing with a blend of nerves and excitement. I have no illusions that this will be easy, but I also know that the path to freedom, to true happiness, is not one I have to walk alone. Not anymore.

With one last look at the quiet chamber, I smile, then push open the door and step into the corridor, ready to find Rian and finally tell him the truth.

THE PATH FROM THE Council House to Rian's castle is long and winding, several hours on foot. Every step along the stone path gives me plenty of time to solidify my decision, to ground myself in the choice I'm about to make, yet my nerves hum in anticipation the entire way. Even knowing what Isabel confessed, my heart flutters like a caged bird, desperate for freedom, yet terrified of the unknown beyond its bars.

The hours melt away as I journey onward, my resolve solidifying with each step. By the time the castle spires come into view against the deepening dusk, I know I'm ready. No more fears. This time, I've truly decided, without hesitation or half-formed plans for escape. The only thing I have left to do is tell Rian exactly how I feel.

I step forward to request entry at the front gate, expecting a warden to come take down the wards, yet no one appears. And none come. I wait, and wait, until I take another step and another until I'm directly in front of the intricate metalwork. My finger trace the iron, hoping the touch will alert whatever watch warden is supposed to be checking the wards. But, to my surprise, the gates swing open and the wards let me through without the slightest hesitation. I take in a trembling breath, wondering if Rian had lowered the wards in hope or if this is just another sign of the depth of his feelings.

Inside the castle, I navigate the familiar halls, the echoes of my own footsteps seeming louder in the empty, evening silence. The familiar tapestries and flickering torchlight blur as I pass, my mind focused solely on what lay ahead. When I reach his quarters, I pause, my hand hovering over the door before I finally gather the courage to knock.

"Enter," comes his muffled voice.

I push open the door, stepping into the warmth of the room. Rian stands by the window, silhouetted by the soft glow of candlelight. His ebony hair is as wild as ever, and it looks as though he hasn't shaved, giving his sharp jawline a shadowed appearance. His surprise at my arrival is evident as he turns, his expression shifting to one of disbelief and a cautious hope as his eyes meet mine.

"Sorcha," he says, his voice holding an edge of wonder. "I didn't expect... I hadn't hoped... I—" He stops himself, a rare moment of flustered silence. "I'm surprised you're here."

"A pleasant surprise, I hope?" I manage, though my voice wavers.

"The best," he murmurs, his gaze intense, almost reverent.

We stand in silence, and though it's charged, it feels vaguely awkward. Finally, I clear my throat and step further into the room. "There's something I need to speak with you about."

His face shudders and he nods, gesturing for me to sit in one of the plush armchairs beside his bed.

I perch on the edge of the seat, twisting my fingers in my lap. The words I practiced in my head now seem tangled and uncertain. "Why didn't you tell me?"

He looks at me, his brows furrowing. "About which part, darling?"

"Changing the tradition, to start. The binding and High King bit." I say, swallowing hard. "Why wouldn't you share your plans with me?"

He studies me, his eyes unreadable before leaning back in his chair. "I had no idea how you'd react, if you'd believe I was trying to pressure you—"

"Yes, telling me you were changing our society's most deeply ingrained laws would pressure me, not like magically binding cuffs we can't escape from."

He has the decency to look chagrined, but only slightly. "It wasn't my best idea."

Looking at it from this side of the story, it wasn't, but it still brought me here. And I can't help but smile at him. "Go on," I prompt.

He takes a slow breath, steadying himself. "I didn't want you to think I was... leveraging my power. If you thought I was changing everything just for you, just to convince you to be with me, I feared you'd feel trapped or indebted. And I couldn't bear that." He pauses, a faint smile tugging at his lips. "Better to let it happen naturally, as a surprise."

"*Were* you doing it for me?" I ask quietly.

He sighs, running a hand through his unruly hair. He looks like both the antlered king I saw in the Council House today and the boy who'd never quite grown up. "I was doing it for everyone, really. We all deserve that choice." He hesitates, lowering his gaze. "But I admit, I didn't want to see you bound again, not when I... not when I hoped..." His words trail off, and he shrugs as if resigned.

I lean forward, studying his face. "And making yourself High King? Did you think I wouldn't find out?" I press, a smile tugging at my lips. "How was I supposed to know you weren't planning to marry someone else?"

A wry smile tugs at his lips. "Can you blame me for being a bit selfish? For wanting you to choose me for me, not for a crown or a kingdom?"

No, I think to myself. *Not when all I wanted was a choice*. And with that, whatever remaining weight I'd been carrying falls away.

"I would have chosen you, had I known you were an option. With or without a crown." Despite myself, a laugh bubbles up. "As if I could ever want you for anything but yourself."

At this, his eyes light up, and he steps forward, kneeling before me. "I suppose," he murmurs, taking my hand in his, "I'd hoped you'd find your way here, before too long."

There's silence as we look at each other, the full weight of what he's done settling around us, its enormity softened by the warmth in his gaze. I take a deep breath, knowing the next question is perhaps the most important of all.

"Why didn't you ever tell me how you felt?" I ask softly, my gaze fixed on him.

Rian's expression shifts, a faint hint of vulnerability there, as he studies me. "Why didn't you?" he counters, his voice low and sincere.

With my free hand, I trace the intricate patterns on the arm of my chair, thinking about all the reasons, the doubts and fears that have held me back. "I was afraid, Rian. I didn't believe... I didn't believe it could be real. That you could feel anything beyond friendship for me."

His gaze softens, and the smile that tugs at his lips is filled with tenderness. "Sorcha, I wanted more than friendship long before I ever knew what to do with that feeling. Do you remember all the wishes you made? Even the smallest ones, when we were younger?" He shakes his head, as if recalling some distant memory. "I wanted so badly to grant them all, to give you whatever you needed. To give you the world."

"Why didn't you?" I ask, that young girl inside me still wounded and wanting to know.

"They weren't the right words," he says, voice thick. "Be with me today, and I could never have you again. Kiss me, just once, and never again. All those lovely wishes would have given me a singular bright moment, and then each would take me away from you."

I bite my lip, remembering what he'd said in Fuil about wishes, how I'd disregarded their seriousness. "Maybe," I begin, "I don't wish anymore. Maybe I can just tell you what I want." Like he'd asked me to do so sincerely when we came together.

A warm smile stretches across his face, a hint of relief mingling with his joy. "I'd like that very much."

I gaze into Rian's beautiful blue eyes, finding a universe of hope and longing reflected back at me. "What I want," I breathe, inching closer, "is you."

Rian's hand tightens around mine. "You have me," he whispers. "You've always had me."

I close the remaining distance between us, my free hand reaching up to cup his cheek. His skin is warm beneath my palm, his stubble scratching gently against my fingertips. Then I press my lips to his in a kiss that's soft, deep, and filled with promise.

His arms come around me, pulling me close, and I can feel the warmth of his body against mine, solid and reassuring. This moment, this choice—my choice—is more real than any magic or crown. It's ours, and that's enough.

Further Reading

If you're interested in more of my writing, check out my website (**kmalady.com**). You can find information about my other projects, like *The Ascend Trials* (a romantic YA portal fantasy all about subverting tropes), *Threads of Fate* (an NA romantic fantasy series adapted from greek myths), and more!

You'll also find bonus chapters in key POVs for various stories!

And if you're looking to spend more time in the trope-ics, check out the below:

<u>SHE WHO FREES THE SELKIE</u>
A sweet romantasy novella with more adventure than intimacy

<u>SHE WHO TURNS THE VAMPIRE</u>
A sweet epistolary romantasy novella

<u>SHE WHO CLAIMS THE ALPHA</u>
A (sweet & spicy) interactive romantasy novella

<u>AND MORE!</u>